Distrust

DeQuindra Renea

COPYRIGHT

ISBN: 069270972X
ISBN-13: 978-0692709726

DEDICATION

This book is dedicated to my beautiful, supportive mother Belinda Johnson Palmer. My love and gratitude for you is something that cannot be put into words. You are my very best friend and I could not imagine my life without you. I am so thankful that I can write about an absent mother although I never had to experience it. No matter what I had to go through you were right by my side. I wish I could share you with the world so every child could experience the love you give me. Thank you a million times! Here's another book for a Ziploc bag! I love you forever and ever and with all my heart!

ACKNOWLEDGMENTS

Every time I finish a book I get a surreal feeling because I'm unable to believe that I actually did it. Being a lover of books since I could read, holding one in my hands with my name on it and flipping through the pages knowing I wrote every word is an absolute blessing. I am so grateful to God, not only for this gift he has given me but for all of the other blessings he showers me with daily. Now that I'm a grown woman I know what it means to say if I had ten thousand tongues I couldn't tell it all and I won't try because I know He already knows, so I'll just say thank you God.

Thanks to my beautiful daughter Nylah for being my motivation and my reason for living. I hope I make you proud.

My father Tony Walker whom I miss dearly. I love you so much. Wish you were here to see me now.

My parents Charles and Belinda Palmer, I love you! I appreciate all you've ever done for me!

My brothers and sisters Shonte', Janelle, Veronica, Tony

Jr., Antonio and Chris I'm so lucky to have you all. Can never express my thanks enough!

Corey Lyons, thank you for the love and support!

To my family and friends, some of my biggest supporters Mel, Antoinette, Chandra, Tiffany, Keisha, Antwan, Netta, Queta, Cierra, Qwanese, Ashley, Whitney, Deborah, Symone, Cynthia, Shannon, Sharonda J., Sharonda C., Alida, Alisha, Shonda, Liana, Nicole, Mya, Jill, Danielle, Delandra, Tari, Valerie and Shirley. Thank you and I love you!`

Special thanks to Carrie Mattern for editing and being absolutely amazing! Dan Waltz for yet another beautiful cover and all of your other help with answering all of my random questions. Couldn't have done it without you two!

I have to thank my city, Flint MI and all of its residents, past and current. I'm praying things get better for us. Only we really know the true beauty, love and talent that Flint has to offer and we will overcome this water situation we just have to keep trusting in God. I love my city and no matter where I go, in my heart Flint will always be home.

Last, but certainly not least, thank you to everyone who purchased or read my very first book Blazing Deception, and to you, the person reading this one! I am so humbly thankful to you and I hope you enjoy my next books just as much as my first! I love you all! Hope you enjoy!

♥ *DeQuindra Renea*

CHAPTER 1

I've never liked older men...yet here I was naked, in my queen sized sleigh bed, with a man old enough to be my father.

What the fuck am I doing? I asked myself as I always did when we were through having sex. This was wrong.

I looked over at Joseph Long: he snored loudly, with his eye lids fluttering indicating he wasn't in a very deep sleep. He had silky, salt and pepper hair that was cut low. My pink and black comforter was pulled up to his chest, covering his naked body. His facial hair was freshly cut in a goatee and his mouth was wide open. Joe was nice looking for his age which was what made me talk to him in the first place, but he was still too old for me.

My phone blared loudly from my nightstand and Kamden's name popped up on the screen. My heart started beating fast. I knew I had to get Joe out immediately. I turned over and he was wide awake, his brown eyes still full of lust as he smiled at me. I smiled back, like the four minutes he had lasted was the very best of my life.

"Naomi, my sweet Naomi," he said grabbing my arms and pulling me close to him. I rolled my eyes behind his back, still letting him cuddle my naked body for a few seconds.

"Okay Joe, you gotta go," I said pushing him away and chuckling at the little rhyme I had made.

"That must've been your little boyfriend calling. What's his name again?"

"His name is none of your damn business. Do I ever ask you how your wife and children are doing?"

Joe sat up and started putting on his clothes. I watched from where I was on my queen-sized bed. He had a nice physique, an athlete's body thanks to his many years of playing college football. Over the years though, he had lost his way to the gym and gained some pounds in the stomach. Typical dad bod. My eyes scanned him as he slid on his black slacks and white button up shirt. Getting out of my bed, I slid on my pink silk robe so I could walk him to the back door.

"You know what I've been thinking?" He asked as he sat on the bed with his back to me putting on his shoes.

"What have you been thinking Joe?"

"About you. You make me feel so alive again… I haven't felt like that in so many years. What if I left my wife? Don't you think you and I could have something beautiful?"

Now Joe was walking towards me, and this time I couldn't hide the look on my face. What Joe and I shared was far from love, and I thought he understood that. His even bringing up the D word was something I never saw coming.

"Shut up Joe. You are not leaving your wife."

"What if I did?" He asked, wrapping his arms around me.

"Joe, come on you gotta leave. I have somewhere I have to be."

He smiled one more time before he grabbed his jacket off of the pink chair in the corner of my room. I followed him down the hallway as he put it on and fixed the collar.

"You got all the bills paid already?"

"Mostly."

"Tell me what you need baby. You know Daddy will take care of it."

I tried not to smile. This was the moment that made all four of those minutes worth it. Joe was generous enough with his money to feed my expensive appetite. He knew I liked nice things and in order to see me, he was going to have to pay to play.

"I need to pay my car note and I need more clothes for work."

"How much is your car note?"

"Three hundred fifty dollars."

Joe reached in his pocket and pulled out his thick wallet. I watched with wide eyes as he thumbed through the bills and pulled out a stack of hundreds.

"This is six, you're gonna have to make that work."

"Six is plenty, thanks Daddy," I said, wrapping my arms around his neck and kissing his cheek. For some reason he liked when I called him that, and I liked to make him happy. The happier he was, the more generous he became.

I walked him to the back door and he gave me a kiss and a

squeeze on the booty before he left and walked to his car that was parked in the lot behind my apartment. Locking the door behind him, I went back into my bedroom and grabbed my phone to return the missed call.

"Hello?" Kamden answered on the second ring.

"Hey, you call me?" I asked pulling the sheets off of my bed.

"Yeah, what were you doing that you couldn't pick up the phone?"

"I was in the shower Kamden, you alright?"

"Yeah, I just been trying to talk to you for the past couple of days and you ain't been having time."

"Kamden, don't start. You know I had to do paperwork for court yesterday."

"And what about the day before that? Hell, what about today?"

I knew what was happening. Kamden was insecure and it was obvious he was feeling like I hadn't been paying him enough attention. It was getting hard to balance this double life, but I couldn't let go of the income that came from Joe.

"Kamden, I don't have time to babysit you. If you missed me so much, why haven't you been to my house to see me in weeks?"

"You don't answer the phone, but you turn it around on me MiMi?"

"Stop calling me MiMi. I have asked you that a thousand times," I said feeling myself getting more annoyed. I sprinkled baby powder on my bed and sprayed some fabric spay on it too before I put on the fresh pink and white cotton sheets.

"Alright, you know what, you call me when you got time for me. Alright *Naomi*."

Kamden had called me by my real name so I knew he was pissed. It didn't even sound right coming out of his mouth. Before I could say another word the call ended and I put my phone back on the nightstand. After folding my bed I went into the bathroom to take a long, hot shower. There was so much going on in my head and since I needed some time to myself I let almost twenty minutes pass before I left the foggy bathroom.

When I got back into my bedroom I had a missed call from my older sister, Shauna. I plopped on my black suede coach and called back.

"You sure do have a problem with answering phone calls lately," Shauna answered.

"Oh shut up, you sound like Kamden. What's up?"

"Nothing, trying to grocery shop but your nephew keeps trying to sneak stuff into my cart. I'm about to put a price tag on him and put him up for sale."

"You better not," I said smiling at the thought of my only nephew Jalil. He was four going on fourteen and I loved him to pieces.

"Well you better come be in line to purchase him. What are you doing?"

"Sitting on the couch watching TV. Joe just left."

"Joe? You're still messing around with that old guy?" She asked and I could almost see her disgusted face through the phone.

"Yeah... And Kamden called when he was here. He's all

pissed because he says I haven't been making time for him."

"And you probably haven't. But you had time to roll around in the sheets with Grandfather Bear."

I couldn't help but let out a laugh.

"Grandfather Bear has a deep wallet. He gave me six hundred dollars when he left. Six hundred dollars! For four minutes Shauna! Name one other thing that can make me that much money in that amount of time."

"You need to stop being so materialistic. Kamden is a nice guy and he does not deserve all that cheatin' bullshit."

"If you remember correctly, Kamden hasn't been a saint."

"But you took him back, and therefore you are supposed to let that stuff go. Joe is a married man and he has children your age. Leave him alone Naomi-nothing good will come of it."

I smacked my lips. Shauna was five years older than me and never let me forget it. It was always just me and her, especially after our mother walked out on us and left us with our father. Shauna looked after me, teaching me what to do when I started my period, combing my hair and picking out my clothes for school, even taking me to get on birth control when I started having sex. She was my rock and although I didn't always like what she said, I usually listened.

"Don't start with me Shauna, let me live my life."

"I'm just saying Naomi, you are such a beautiful young woman. You don't need to be selling your body like some two dollar hoe to make a couple of extra dollars. I've seen you with Kamden. I've seen the way he looks at you and we both know he makes you happy. He has changed you in ways I never thought possible. I want happiness for you Naomi, and I think Kamden will give you that."

I didn't say anything because I knew it was always best to let Shauna talk. She did have me thinking though. Kamden and I had been through a lot, but he had really been trying to make me happy. Now, it seemed like I was letting him down.

I let Shauna lecture me for a while longer about what decisions I should make in my life before she continued her grocery shopping. I had some thinking to do, so I kicked back in my living room and watched reality TV to make me feel better about my mess of a life.

The cat fights and drink throwing of reality TV was entertaining for a few hours, but I was ready to cuddle. I picked up my phone to call Kamden until I remembered he was mad at me. I had given him enough time to cool down and now it was time for some make up sex. Turning off my TV I threw on some clothes, grabbed my purse and keys and headed to his house.

I didn't expect Kamden to be any different than he was when he got mad at me every other time. I knocked softly on the front door and waited a few minutes before Kamden finally opened it. He was in his underwear, revealing all of his smooth, light brown skin. He looked down at me, his 6'2" frame towering over me since I was only 5'3". He had light brown eyes, and black hair that was cut into a fade. With no facial hair at all, he had a baby face, but what I loved most about him were his big, juicy lips. He bit the bottom one as he glared at me. He didn't look happy to see me at all, but I knew he would be when he saw what I had in store for him.

"Hey baby," I said softly, giving him a sexy smile.

His expression didn't change.

"What you doin' here Naomi, it's like midnight."

"I know. What, I'm not allowed to come see you?"

"You can, I just didn't think you had time these days."

"Kamden," I said softly, unable to believe he was still mad. "I'm sorry."

He laughed.

"You're sorry? No you not Naomi, you're sneaky! That's what you are!"

"What? How am I sneaky?"

"You want me to believe you haven't been answering my calls because you been busy with work? No, you been busy getting fucked, that's what you been doing."

I shook my head. Kamden and I both had been unfaithful in the past, and it was something neither of us seemed to be able to get over. Anytime I didn't answer the phone he thought I was with somebody else. Our three year relationship was falling apart, and it wasn't until today when I'd talked to Shauna, that I realized I didn't want that to happen.

"Are you really going to make me stand out here on the porch Kamden?" I asked after a few minutes. He stood aside and opened the door allowing me to walk in.

"What's going on with us Kamden?" I asked, sitting on the sofa. "What are we doing? Do you want to be with me or not?"

"I should be asking you that MiMi. I've been trying to be with you and spend time with you. It's you that doesn't have time for me."

"I said sorry Kam."

Kamden just sat there and shook his head. I didn't know what was happening, but this what not how I imagined my night would go.

"I still love you MiMi, but it's not working out. I'm not getting what I need from you and it's obvious you don't care."

"Kamden, are you serious? You really breaking up with me?"

"Yeah MiMi, I really am. I'm tired of the back and forth same old bullshit."

I didn't say anything else. If Kamden thought I was about to beg him to be with me he had another thing coming. I was a bad bitch and could find another Kamden around the corner anyway... at least that's what I told myself. Nodding my head I walked away slowly, expecting him to come after me or call me back. When I heard the door slam though, I knew he was serious. I wanted to go back and apologize, but my pride led me back to my car and home to my empty apartment.

CHAPTER 2

"Naomi, really? You're really not on your way?" my best friend Kapri asked as I slid into my red pumps and grabbed my keys.

"I am walking out the door right now Kapri-I swear."

"Hurry up. I don't wanna go in there and meet them by myself. You better not be standing me up. I know you don't really wanna go."

"I wouldn't do you like that. Just let him know this is not a double date-I'm only going to meet your friend and make you feel comfortable."

"I know I told him. Thank you Naomi," she sang.

"You're welcome. Now let me check my make up and walk out the door."

"Okay, see you in a minute, and be careful."

Ending the call, I looked at myself in the mirror. It had been almost a week since Kamden had broken up with me and although I wasn't trying to show it, I was hurting. Kamden was the person I loved and I had always thought I would spend the rest of my life with. It seemed being with Joe only made me miss him more. The worse part about our breakup was I didn't see it coming. So tonight, although this wasn't officially a date, it was definitely a little black dress occasion. Mine was short and strapless, and I had on a pair of red pumps that made me look two inches taller. My newly streaked burgundy hair, which was flat ironed and hung down my back, brought out the red eye shadow I had applied along with my signature ruby lipstick. I looked damn good, and if nothing else, somebody was going to buy me a drink and tell me what a fool Kamden was when he let me go.

When I arrived at Lucky's Lounge, Kapri was already sitting with two gentlemen at the bar. One was tall and dark with a bald head and big brown eyes. He was muscular like a body builder, and I knew right away he was Kapri's new boo. He was totally her type: all looks and little brains. The other was short, but still a couple inches taller than me in my heels. He had honey brown skin like me, and braids that hung to his back. He was definitely cute, but I wasn't in the mood to get anything started with anybody new. I would flirt and talk, only because that's what I liked to do when I was at the bar, but I knew it wouldn't go any further than that.

"Naomi! Hey girl," Kapri said waving me over. I approached them and gave her a hug. She looked flawless in her gold and black one strap dress and gold stilettos. Her hair was pulled into a curly ponytail and she had on large, gold earrings and a gold necklace.

"You look amazing!" She exclaimed as she hugged me. "Thank you again."

"No problem, you know I got you girl."

"This is my friend Brock," she said introducing me to the dark skinned, muscular guy. "And this is his cousin Rashad. Guys, this is my best friend, Naomi."

"Hi, nice to meet you," I said shaking both of their hands. The first thing I noticed was Rashad's gray, bedroom eyes. I was a sucker for guys with pretty eyes.

I sat between Kapri and Rashad and ordered a martini. It was the night of a big football game and the bar was packed. There was a lot of eye candy in there and despite my feelings, I was glad I went ahead and got dressed up.

"So how long you and Kapri been friends?"

"About ten years now," I said sipping my drink.

"She told me you didn't wanna come out tonight, but I'm glad you did. You look damn sexy," he whispered in my ear softly.

"Thank you."

"Why didn't you wanna come out? You didn't wanna meet me?" he asked with a fake pout on his face. I laughed.

"My boyfriend just broke up with me."

"He broke up with you? You must be one of them fine ass crazy women, huh?"

"No, I don't think I'm crazy," I laughed again. "I guess we are just in different places."

"He shouldn't give up on you so easy," he said glaring at my body. "You're sexy as hell. I know Kapri said you didn't come here on no romantic shit, but I don't think I can let you leave without getting your number or something. You ain't about to just slide away."

I gave him a sexy smile but didn't say anything, and took a sip of my martini. I was having a good time with Rashad and keeping my mind off of Kamden. I was also closely watching the interaction between Kapri and Brock. She was my best friend and seeing how he treated her in public was going to be another factor that would determine whether or not I approved.

I sat and talked to Rashad for about an hour and ordered another martini. He was hilarious, and kept me laughing. Kapri seemed to be enjoying herself too. Brock and Kapri were hugged up and kissing and the night was going well. I'd been at the bar for almost two hours when my phone blared from inside my purse. After digging it out, I was surprised to see Kamden's name.

"Excuse me for a minute Rashad, I need to take this," I said grabbing my purse, leaving the bar, and stepping into the ladies bathroom.

"Hello?"

"Where are you?"

I smacked my lips and rolled my eyes as if he was standing in front of me.

"What do you want Kamden? Why are you calling me?"

"You just couldn't wait to go out on a date with your new dude, huh? I know you and Kapri at Lucky's Lounge with some dudes."

"Why the hell are you spying on me? And what do you care, you broke up with me remember? We're done."

Kamden didn't say anything for a minute.

"You know I aint mean that shit MiMi."

"I don't care. If you didn't mean it, you shouldn't have said it."

"Baby… Who is this dude you at the bar with for real? You been fuckin' him?"

"Kamden, I'm done talking about this. Goodbye."

"MiMi, you give my pussy to somebody else I swear we will be done forever."

"You gonna threaten me after you broke up with me? You said you were done. I gave you three years of my life and just like that, you're done with me for no reason? Fuck you Kamden."

I ended the call and put my phone back in my purse. I had no clue how Kamden knew where I was and I didn't give a damn either. He could have spies in my panties if he wanted to. Since they were watching, I would make sure to give them something to run back and tell.

When I got back to the bar Kapri and Brock were still hugged up and Rashad was drinking his beer and watching the game. I climbed back in the barstool and asked the bartender to pour out my old drink and bring me a new one. One thing Shauna had taught me was to never drink something once I'd left it at the table. I turned to Rashad and smiled.

"I'm sorry about that," I said.

"It's cool. Everything alright?"

"Yeah, just my sister. I was making sure she made it home safely from dropping my nephew off to his father," I lied.

"So you got a sister?"

"Yeah, just one. She's older, and I'm better looking," I

joked.

"I bet you are. So have you changed your mind yet?"

"About what?"

"Letting me have your number," he said smiling. "You know I wanna see you again."

"I don't know Rashad, you know I just got out of a relationship."

"I'm not trying to tie you down, just take you out and show you a good time."

I shrugged my shoulders.

"We'll see."

I winked my eye at him to let him know there was still hope. He was cute and I liked him, but I couldn't get Kamden off of my mind, especially now that he had called me. I checked my phone and I had a missed text message. I knew it was from Kamden before I even looked at it.

You better not leave with him. And don't make me come up there.

He was really acting crazy. How the hell could he be saying all this to me after he broke up with me? As far as I was concerned we were through.

Stop texting me Kamden. You said we were through, so we're through, I replied. I put my phone back in my purse and gave Rashad my undivided attention. I didn't care if Kamden texted me back because there wasn't anything else to talk about. He already knew I wasn't the type of girl to let loose, and now that he'd done that, he would have to deal with the consequences.

After about another hour of drinking and trying to sober up with glasses of water, I was ready to head home. Rashad paid for my drinks and offered to walk me to the car. I accepted thinking it would be a good show for Kamden's punk ass spies.

"Thanks again for paying for my drinks. And for keeping me company."

"Nah, you kept me company. I was a third wheel before you came in and took my breath away."

I smiled again and blushed unwillingly. Rashad was hilarious and sweet, but I didn't want to give him false hopes. I was glad when he opened the door and bid me goodnight without asking for my phone number again. If things worked out between Kapri and Brock, we would see each other again. I started my car, turned on my music and headed home, watching Rashad go back into the bar in my rearview mirror.

As I pulled up to my apartment I was comfortable and vibing so good to the music I didn't even want to get out of the car. I grabbed my purse and the bag of Tim Hortons I'd stopped and gotten and headed into my apartment.

"So straight up, as soon as we break up you gonna go out on a date," I heard Kamden say from behind me. I turned around and there he was walking towards me wearing a pair of jean shorts and a NCAA t-shirt.

"Kamden? What the fuck- you scared the hell outta me," I said, putting my hand on my chest. "Why are you here? And who lied and told you I was on a date?"

"Nobody lied, I know you was at the bar with some dude," he said walking up on me.

"Yeah I was, so what? It wasn't a date, and anyway I don't owe you an explanation for anything. I'm single now in case you forgot."

Kamden bit his lip which meant he was beyond pissed off. I turned around and proceeded to walk into my apartment making sure to put a little extra switch in my walk because I knew he was watching. I didn't turn around, but I could hear him behind me, walking to my apartment as if he was welcome inside.

"Go home Kamden," I said over my shoulder. My knees were shaking like they always did when Kamden was around. He couldn't know that though. I had to let him know I was not one he could drop and pick back up when he was afraid somebody else was coming along.

Kamden didn't respond, just continued to follow me to my apartment. I unlocked my door, and tried to close it behind me, but he was too strong. He pushed his way inside and locked the door behind us.

"Didn't I say go home Kamden? I don't wanna talk to you."

I went into the kitchen and took my muffin out of the bag. That was the last thing I was going to say to him. If I ignored him and acted like he wasn't there, eventually he would leave.

"I aint going nowhere until we talk."

I took a bite out of the top of my muffin making sure my mouth was full so there was no way I could respond. He waited for me to chew, and I did, but still didn't say anything to him.

"The other night I was pissed off. You been acting like you don't got time for me and you know how I am. I get to thinking you with somebody else. I don't want you with anybody else."

Kamden came into the kitchen and sat at one of the stools at the island. Grabbing my hand, he pulled me onto his lap.

"Tell me his name... The guy you were with at the bar."

"I don't remember," I lied. "I was only going because this was Kapri's first date with her boo and she didn't want to go alone."

Kamden moved my hair aside and started kissing my neck.

"He try to get your number?"

"Yeah," I moaned. I tried not to like it, but Kamden knew what turned me on. He knew exactly what buttons to push and when to push them. He ran his hands down the front of my dress and used both of his hands to spread my legs. The muffin I'd been eating didn't taste good anymore. Now, I only wanted one thing in my mouth and it didn't have chocolate chips in it.

"Did you give it to him?" He asked moving, my panties to the side. He slid one finger between my pussy lips and let it rest right at my opening.

"No," I shook my head. "I should've," I said as an afterthought.

"Oh yeah," Kamden said standing up and lifting me off of my feet. He pushed everything on my island to the side and sat me on it. "Why is that?"

"Because I'm single."

"Single? You think so?"

I nodded my head.

"I know so."

"So what if I fuck the single out of you... Then what? You'll be mine again?"

I smiled. Kamden loved talking shit and I did too. I knew he wanted me... he always threw a tantrum when he did. The breakup was his way of getting my attention, but it backfired when I acted as if I didn't give a damn. Pissing him off was about to make this sex so much better.

"Once you drop Naomi you don't get a chance to pick her back up again. It's game time until somebody else gets the ball," I said.

Kamden put his hands under my dress again and slid my panties down.

"Keep telling me how you gonna get somebody else. I wanna remember it so I can remind you when you screaming my name once I'm done."

I knew he wasn't lying. Kamden knew how to lay it down, that's why I was so pissed when he'd given it away to some other bitch. It didn't matter, because nobody had pussy better than Naomi Duncan and Kamden was living proof of that because he always came back, and here he was again.

I laid back on my elbows as Kamden put my legs into the air. He played with me for a minute sliding his fingers between my pussy and all the way back to my anus repeatedly. When he spread my legs again, I knew he could see the mess his fingers alone had created.

My eyes watched intently as he went into my refrigerator, got some whipped cream and sat back down on the stool and let my legs rest on his shoulders. I could hear the whooshing of the can of whipped cream before I felt the cold substance hit my clit and I squirmed to get away. He grabbed my hips and pulled me back down on his face licking the whipped cream of slowly.

"Mmmmm," I moaned as I pulled my dress up over my head. The only thing I was wearing now were my red pumps. I could hear Kamden slurping and felt his spit mixed with my juices traveling down the crack of my ass. He lifted me up and licked from my behind all the way back up to my opening and put his tongue inside. I moaned again, but bit my lip to keep myself from saying his name. It was feeling so good that my eyes were in the back of my head and I was grinding on his tongue.

"You taste better than the whipped cream," he said standing up and pushing his face in deeper.

"Oh! Yesssss...."

Kamden sucked on my clit one last time and came up to give me a kiss on the lips.

"I love your mean ass and you know I do," he said putting his tongue in my mouth. I sucked on it slow, the same way he had done my clit before I pushed him away.

I didn't say anything, just unbuttoned his jean shorts and pulled them down until I heard them hit the floor. He stood before me wearing only his t-shirt and a pair of gray and black boxers. I bit my lip as I pulled off his clothes, first his shirt, then his boxers. His penis was hard and pointing right at me. I smiled as I took it in my mouth.

"Damn... Baby," he said as he grabbed my head and

pulled my hair back. "I love when you suck it like that…like you missed it. Did you miss me baby?"

I nodded my head as I continued to suck on his dick slowly, taking as much of it as I could into my mouth. He moaned in a way that made me hot all over and I played with myself to make sure that I stayed nice and wet for him.

"Suck it like that baby, don't stop," he said. I looked up at him as he stood, his knees weak and eyes closed. Relaxing my throat, I took all of him in my mouth before he abruptly pulled my head away like he was taking a lollipop out of my mouth.

"You too good baby," he said shaking his head. "Tryna make me cum all quick."

I laughed and shook my head as he pushed me back on the counter. He positioned himself between my legs and looked me in my eyes as he slid himself inside of me.

"What's my name?" He asked, biting his lip but this time I knew he wasn't mad because he was smiling with pleasure. I shook my head because I wasn't about to give up that easy. He thrust himself so deep inside of me I thought I could feel it in my stomach. I screamed out in pleasure, but I still didn't say his name. My breasts bounced as he continued to stroke in and out of me and he reached out to grab them.

"Come on baby, say my name," he whispered, playing with my brown nipples. He leaned down and took one into his mouth. I moaned, but still didn't say his name.

All of a sudden Kamden picked me up, his penis still deep inside of me. He put my back against the wall and held on to me tight as he pulled me down on his dick repeatedly. I couldn't stop screaming now because he was hitting my spot.

"Say... my... name," he said into my ear as I began to grind trying to reach that orgasm I could feel building inside of me. Kamden didn't give me a chance to respond before he pulled me down again.

"Yes! Ohmy-"

I couldn't finish my sentence because Kamden was gently biting my neck and I couldn't take it anymore.

"Kamden! Kamden! Oh my God, I love you! Please don't stop!"

I used the wall as leverage and held onto his shoulders as I bounced up and down on his dick as the feeling of pure ecstasy overtook my body. My body became limp for a minute as Kamden carried me back over to the counter.

"Uh uh, we aint done yet. Get on your knees," he ordered.

I turned over on the counter and got on my knees, sticking my butt high in the air so Kamden would have easy access. Before he entered me, he got on his knees and began to eat my pussy from behind. Using his tongue like a dick he pushed in and out of me. Just as I was about to cum a second time, he replaced his tongue with his penis and played with my nipples from the back.

"You so sexy baby. Damn, I love you so much."

"I love you too," I whispered with my eyes closed, already trying to reach my second orgasm. Kamden was the only man I had ever met that could make me cum multiple times in different positions. I knew with him I would never be disappointed.

"I love you too baby, so much. Keep riding it like that

baby, I'm about to cum," he said into my ear. I threw it back at him as hard as I could until he got a look of extreme pleasure on his face. We took a minute to catch our breath before we went upstairs to take a hot shower. Exhausted, we both climbed in bed naked, warm and fresh.

CHAPTER 3

"Do you love me?"

Kamden asked me that early the next morning waking me out of my sleep. I was lying on his chest and he was running his fingers through my hair. The sun was starting to come up providing a dim natural light to my bedroom.

"You know I love you Kam," I said half asleep. "Why are you asking me that?"

"Because I wanna know."

"If I didn't you wouldn't be here naked in my bed right now. Nobody gets to just break up with me then come have sex."

"I didn't break up with you, I was just pissed. You got a careless attitude sometimes and it makes me crazy. But you know I aint never going nowhere."

Kamden wrapped his arms around me and kissed me on the forehead. It was times like this when I knew there was no other place I belonged. Kamden was the man I wanted to marry and create a family with. Our relationship was so up and down though; I didn't really have the faith we would make it that far. Both of us wanted commitment, but neither of us wanted to be faithful. At the end of the day though, I had his heart and he had mine and that's what made leaving each other so hard.

Kamden's phone blared from wherever it was on the floor. I may have been half asleep, but my eyes popped open when I heard that.

"Who's calling you this early?"

"How could I know that when I'm in the bed with you?"

I didn't say anything for a minute, just closed my eyes.

"Do you love me? That's the question," I asked after a little while of thinking.

"Why is that the question?"

"Because... of past situations."

Kamden took a deep breath before he answered.

"I knew you was gonna bring that Rebecca shit up."

"Don't call it shit Kamden, and don't try to turn over. I asked you a question."

"Look baby. I can understand why you feel so insecure about us. I fucked up real bad in the past and I know I have to make that right with you, but you also have to try to trust me."

"You still haven't answered my question Kamden," I said, trying to bring him back to what I had asked in the first place.

"You already know I love you MiMi, I can't never let you go."

I paused before I asked my next question because I didn't

want to ruin the moment.

"If you love me so much how can you carry on a relationship with somebody else at the same time you're with me?"

Kamden took a deep breath and tried to turn over.

"I know we aint talkin' about this Rebecca shit again."

"Yes we are talking about this Rebecca shit again, and don't try to pull away from me."

"MiMi look, me being with you and Rebecca at the same time had nothing to do with you or my love for you. I was being selfish. And once it all blew up in my face, I knew I had to let Rebecca go. Losing you wasn't even an option."

My heart did flips when he said that, but I still had more questions.

"So you don't talk to her anymore?"

He didn't answer or look at me, just shook his head. I knew he was tired of me talking about Rebecca and questioning him about her, but this all had just happened less than a year ago. It was still fresh and it still hurt, and since he was the one responsible for it he didn't have a choice.

The more I thought about him and Rebecca and the pain I felt when I found out about it, the more questions I had. It wasn't like this was some girl he had just smashed and moved on, he had celebrated anniversaries and met her family! All of the special things he was doing with me he was doing with her also.

"What you did with her makes me feel insecure. I don't feel like we shared anything special, or that our relationship had an impact on you because you were focused on somebody else most of the time."

Kamden nodded his head.

"I get it baby. And I wish there was something I could do to take that away, or make you secure in knowing every moment I shared with you was special, that's why I'm with you. I can only tell you with all my heart that there is nothing Rebecca has that I want anymore. It's all about you now and forever MiMi… only you."

Kamden pulled me as close as he could to his naked body and kissed me on the forehead. Everything in my heart was telling me Kamden was being honest, so instead of questioning him more I closed my eyes and went to sleep, thankful to be in the arms of the love of my life.

When we woke up a few hours later, we took a shower together and got dressed. We couldn't stop kissing and hugging each other. I was happy Kamden had come over and that we were back together.

I cleaned my counter before I made us a quick egg and bacon sandwich. Kamden came downstairs dressed in some sweatpants and a shirt from the drawer he had in my room.

"I hope you made me something or I'm eating yours," he said entering the kitchen.

"I did."

I put the sandwich in front of him and sat across the table.

"So…about last night…"

A big smile spread across Kamden's face.

"Yeah, about it. Whose name did you end up screaming?"

"Yours… but that's not what I want to talk to you about."

"What's up?" he asked, taking a bite of his breakfast sandwich.

"What are we really doing Kamden?"

"What you mean?"

I took a deep breath before I started. I really didn't wanna bring such a serious situation up because we had spoke briefly last night, but I wanted to have a clear understanding of where I stood in Kamden's life and his late night phone call was still unsettling to me.

"I mean you say you want to be with me, but you're not faithful. You get calls in the middle of the night... I just want to understand. If you're not ready to be committed to me, just go ahead and say it. We can still be friends."

"So because somebody calls me early in the morning, I'm being unfaithful?"

"At booty call hours, yes."

"It could've been my Momma."

"If it was, I'm sure you would've tried to answer it. Don't play me Kamden, tell me the truth."

"You already know what the truth is MiMi, that's why I came last night. If I didn't love you I could've handled you being out on a date with some dude-"

"It wasn't a date."

"-thinking about you with somebody else wouldn't bother me if I didn't love you. I know what I want, and I know who I want and I know that person is you."

I wanted to smile, but I had to keep a stone face. Kamden was good with words and he knew how to make me feel like I was the only girl in his world, even when I wasn't. He'd done it the whole second year of our relationship, carrying on a full blown relationship with another girl named Rebecca a few hours away while I was turning down men trying to stay faithful.

"You are the person I want to meet my family and that I want to love for the rest of my life. I know I've made mistakes before and I haven't been faithful, but I don't wanna play them games anymore MiMi. I wanna love your forever. So what's up between us is I'm yours and you're mine."

Kamden got up from his seat and I thought he was about to get down on one knee, but he came over and gave me a deep kiss on the lips.

"You really want me to meet your family?" I asked happily. He nodded his head and I jumped up and threw my arms around him. What he was saying was everything I had been waiting for and a sign that our relationship was definitely moving forward. This made me happy. I needed Kamden, even though he was like a bad habit. I knew I couldn't be honest with him about what I'd done because it would ruin everything, so I made a silent promise to myself that I would be faithful to him from this point forward.

CHAPTER 4

With everything going on in my life, I was long overdue for a girl's night. Although I had my mind made up about the status of our relationship, I wanted to get the opinion of those closest to me so I invited Shauna, Kapri and my favorite cousin, Tarrissa, over to get their opinion. They knew everything I had been through with Kamden and they would keep it real with me. I had to admit I felt like a fool because I was once again telling them I was taking Kamden back, but they would find out eventually anyway.

I had gone to the grocery store earlier that day to get wine, fruit and cheese, and I'd also made some nacho dip. After lighting candles and turning on music, I waited for my guests to arrive. Always punctual, Shauna was first. Everybody said we looked alike because of our similar features: light brown skin, slanted gray eyes like our father, and button noses. Shauna's hair was cut into a bob and newly colored copper, complimenting her skin tone.

"Hi Sissy Pooh!" She exclaimed as soon as she let herself in with the key. She claimed I took too long to answer the door.

"Hi big Sissy! I missed you!"

We hugged and she didn't waste any time helping herself to some wine and nachos.

"So, it's been a while since we've had a girl's night... what's going on?"

"Why does something have to be going on for me to have a girl's night?"

Shauna shrugged her shoulders.

"Just asking."

"I just missed my girls."

"Who's all coming?"

"Just you, Tarrissa, and Kapri."

Shauna rolled her eyes. She had never been a big fan of Kapri.

"Be nice," I said with pleading eyes. Anybody who thought I was hot-headed had not encountered my sister and I did not want my relaxing girls night to turn into an episode of reality TV.

"I'm always nice, just tell her to watch her step."

"She'll be fine."

Shauna and I chatted for awhile about her life and Jalil's latest antics before there was a knock at my door. Tarrissa was there with a pot of her apple crisp I loved so much. I greeted her with a big kiss on the cheek.

"Did you bring this for me? Rissa, you shouldn't have."

"Well I did want everybody to have some too. Put up some for later."

Tarrissa was the daughter of my father's only sister. Since

our mother walked out on us, our Aunt Sueann was the only mother figure we had in our lives so Shauna and I grew up close with her daughter. She was short like me with copper skin, brown eyes and high cheekbones. Her hair was in a cute, curly mini-fro and she wore gold, dangling earrings. Tarrissa gave Shauna a hug and kiss before she got a plate and glass of wine of her own.

"What were ya'll talking about before I got here?" Tarissa asked, taking a bite of a tortilla chip drizzled with cheese.

"My son and his latest tricks. You know he is always up to something."

"Jalil is going to be the CEO of a big company one day."

"You always say that."

"Since the day I laid eyes on him and I'm going to keep saying it. I'm telling you he is going to be filthy rich."

"Good then- he can take care of his Momma."

"And his Auntie," I added taking a sip of my wine.

"And me. Hell, I'm the one that spoke it into existence," Tarrissa said.

"What's been going on with you? Anybody new in your life we need to know about?" I asked Tarrissa. She rolled her eyes and went through her mental black book to see if there was somebody she hadn't given us the details on. Tarrissa was like me, she had no problems keeping company; the only difference was she preferred the company of females.

"Leslie is who I've been dealing with the most. I'm trying to stay away from her, but she's falling for me."

"And? Are the feelings mutual?"

"I don't know. My heart still belongs to Sabrina and it's

hard to move on."

"Tarrissa, Sabrina left you over two years ago. I don't wanna tell you get over it but baby… get over it," Shauna said. I smacked her on the arm.

"Shauna stop that. It's not easy to move on from somebody you love. There is no time limit."

"Fuck that, when I left Jason's ass I had another boyfriend by the end of the month. Life is too short to be dwelling on one person."

Tarrissa and I both shook our head just as there was another knock on the door. Shauna immediately rolled her eyes already knowing who was on the other side.

"Shauna," I said in a warning tone.

"Okay, I know I'll be nice."

"What?" Tarrissa asked confused, looking from Shauna to me for an explanation.

"You know she hates Kapri," I whispered as I walked to the door.

"Why? I like Kapri," Tarrissa said. Neither of us got a chance to respond because Kapri was walking through the door dressed in yoga pants and a pink hoodie.

"Hey girl, how are you?" I asked giving her a hug.

"I'm good. You look cute as usual. Hi Rissa, hey Shauna," she said waving at my sister and cousin. They both returned, hi, politely, as I sat back down and Kapri went into the kitchen to get a glass of wine and something to eat.

"So what were we talking about?" I asked, picking my glass up off of the table.

"Shauna being a hoe," Tarrissa joked.

"I am not a hoe, I just don't like being alone. Commitment is better for me. I'm a relationship girl. I'm not like Naomi, I don't like being single."

"Who said I liked being single?"

"Your actions. Admit it, you can't be faithful... and as soon as things are getting really serious you start acting crazy so he'll break up with you," Shauna answered.

"Well speaking of commitment... I'm really gonna do it this time."

"Do what?" Kapri asked sitting next to Tarrissa on the loveseat.

"Be committed. Kamden came over the other night and we made up. He said I'm the one he wants to be with and that he loved me. He even asked me to go to meet his family."

"Yes!" Shauna said throwing her hands up in the air. "I'm sorry, but ya'll already know I've always been team Kamden."

"I like Kamden too I guess," Kapri said. "But after everything you've been through with him, can you really trust him?"

"I was thinking that too, but he seems different this time like he really wants to do things right."

"That's what he always says when he wants to get you back," Kapri said. "Whatever you decide to do, I'm happy for you- I just don't trust him."

Kapri always told me the cold truth which was why I kept her around. Sometimes you needed that one friend that was willing to hurt your feelings a little to wake you up.

"I don't think one more chance can hurt, especially

because I know you love Kamden. If you leave him and get with somebody else you might end up going through the same thing anyway. Might as well be with someone you know truly loves you," Tarrissa said. Kapri made a noise and a face as she took a sip of her wine.

"Is there something you need to say Kapri?" Shauna asked defensively.

"I'm not saying he doesn't love her," Kapri explained. "It's just funny that when they break up he all of a sudden wants her again as soon as he finds out she's seeing someone else. Is it really the fact that he loves you, or is it that he doesn't want anybody else to have you?"

I didn't know how to answer that question because Kapri was exactly right. Every time we broke up and I started seeing someone else, Kamden all of a sudden couldn't live without me. I'd planned the girl's night to hear all of their opinions. I didn't really think they would have me second guessing my decision.

"So what, are ya'll saying I shouldn't be committed to Kamden?"

"You should do what makes you happy," Shauna said before anyone could open their mouths. That was her way of telling me she was my big sister and therefore I should listen to her.

"Agreed," Tarrissa said getting strawberries off the platter. Nobody knows what your relationship is like but you… and you're the one that's going to have to live with it."

I looked at Kapri and waited for her to answer. She responded with a bright smile.

"You know what you feel Naomi. If Kamden makes you happy, give it your all. You know I'm always here for you."

I pulled out a fifth of Patron and poured all of the girls a shot in my cute little leopard shot glasses.

"I knew there was a reason for this girls night you sneaky little heffah," my sister said nudging me. We raised our shots and toasted to mind blowing sex, good health, faithful relationships, and lots of money.

I awoke in the middle of the night to my phone blaring from my dining room table. Shauna was asleep on the couch with me, Tarrissa had grabbed a pillow and was lying on the floor, and Kapri was asleep in the recliner. I stumbled as quietly and quickly as I could over to the table to answer it before it woke any of the girls, not that they had stirred anyway. When I saw Joe's name on my screen I almost didn't answer it, but there was no use in avoiding anybody. The sooner I told Joe the truth, the sooner he would stop calling and I could focus all of my attention on Kamden.

"Hello?"

"What's up pretty girl, you sleep?" He asked in a whisper.

"Yeah, I was. How you doin' Joe?"

"I'm alright. Missin' you."

"You don't miss me Joe."

"I do! I miss your face. I miss those meals you cook me. I miss holding you. I miss you Naomi. Why don't you believe me?"

"Because you have a wife. Where is she right now?"

"Since when do you start asking questions about my wife?"

I didn't answer right away, just went and put the leftover fruit in the refrigerator.

"Naomi? What's wrong? What did I do?"

"You didn't do anything Joe, I just can't see you anymore."

"Can't see me? Why? Because of my wife?"

"No, because I... just can't. You should focus on your wife and kids, your family. Focus on what's important."

"You don't think you fit in that category baby? My wife doesn't make me happy like you do. She doesn't do the things to me that you do."

"Joe, I can't-"

"Please let me come see you Naomi. Don't tell me that we're through like this."

"This isn't a relationship Joe," I said sitting on my kitchen counter and talking as quietly as I could. "But I am in one and I can't do this anymore."

"So that's what this is about, your little boyfriend?"

"Yeah," I said rolling my eyes. He was dragging this out longer than the thirty second conversation I'd rehearsed in my head.

"So it's no purpose in us talking about it because this is what it's going to be. I truly wish the best to you and your family."

I didn't wait for Joe to say anything else, I just ended the call. I knew I was doing the right thing. Joe was married like I planned on being one day. The last thing I wanted was karma coming back one day and giving me what I deserved.

"So, you're letting Grandaddy go, huh?" Shauna said,

coming into the kitchen.

"Shauna! You scared the fuck out of me. Why are you sneaking up on me and ear hustling?"

"Well I tried my best not to listen, but it was like the heavens wanted me to hear so I could tell you that you're doing the right thing."

""Well tell the heavens I said thank you," I teased. "What are you doing up anyway?"

"I was on my way to your bed."

"My bed. That's where you think you're sleeping?"

"Absolutely. I'll be damned if I get a backache sleeping on that couch. You know I'm frail."

"Well wake Rissa up and tell her to get on the couch… it's better than that floor."

Shauna nodded and I lazily cleaned the kitchen before heading upstairs to my bed. I lay beside my sister and we talked and laughed until we fell asleep, just like we did when we were kids.

CHAPTER 5

Meeting Kamden's mother was the scariest thing ever. I had butterflies in my stomach for days before we actually met. I was twenty-two years old and had never been in a real relationship where I went home to meet the family. I didn't know what I should wear or say, but Kamden was excited. He said he wanted to show me off and prove to me that he was serious about taking our relationship to the next level.

When the day arrived, I couldn't stay out of the mirror checking my makeup and clothes. I wanted to make a good impression on Kamden's mother... I wanted her to really like me. By the time Kamden got to my apartment, I was on pins and needles, pacing.

"Baby," he said grabbing my face and making me look in his eyes. "Calm down, you do not need to be this nervous, it's just my Momma."

"I know, but I want her to like me."

"Everybody likes you MiMi."

"Don't call me that Kam, how many times do I have to

ask you?"

Kamden kissed my lips and went into the kitchen.

"You got some food? I'm hungry."

"We're not eating at your Momma's house?"

Kamden laughed.

"My mom don't cook."

"Well in that case, there should be some leftover meatloaf and mashed potatoes in the refrigerator. Warm some up for me too."

My nerves hadn't gotten any better by the time we pulled up to Kamden's mother's house. It was small, but in a nice neighborhood where kids were playing outside and everyone made sure their yards looked nice. Kamden held my hand tightly as he knocked on the door. He put my hair behind my ear and gave me a kiss while we waited, and when she came to the door, my mouth almost hit the floor.

The woman standing in front of me was not what I had prepared for. His mother looked younger than me, and was wearing short, tight, blue jean shorts and a yellow tank top with no bra. She had short, brown hair and brown eyes. She was a pretty woman, just not what I had expected. Kamden looked embarrassed and didn't waste any time voicing his disapproval.

"Ma, I told you we would be here around four, why you ain't dressed?"

"I am dressed Kamden, don't come in here with all that. Is this MiMi?"

"Yes ma'am," I said politely, not bothering to correct her.

She wrapped her arms around me.

"It is so nice to finally meet you. I have been asking and asking Kamden to bring you over here. He talks about you all the time."

"Ma, that's enough."

"No it's not," I joked. She laughed.

"Well my name is Roxanne, come on in. Hi baby," she said hugging and kissing Kamden as if he was a three year old.

"Momma, you should've put a bra on, come on. And why you ain't clean up?"

His mother's house wasn't junky, but it wasn't the cleanest either. There were piles of clothes in the middle of the floor like she had been sorting laundry and a couple of used cups and beer cans lying around. She moved a stack of newspapers from the couch so we would have room to sit down.

"Kamden, am I your Momma or are you my father? Because the last time I checked, I gave birth to you and you don't pay my bills. Don't get embarrassed in front of your pretty girlfriend."

Kamden sat on the couch next to me and put his arm around me.

"So MiMi, explain to me how you can be dating my son for three years without meeting me."

"Well, Kamden and I haven't had the easiest relationship. I guess he didn't want us to meet until he knew he was ready to commit."

"And that's what you're doing? Because I'm not trying to rush things, but it's about time I had a grandbaby."

"Well, nobody's getting pregnant tomorrow Ma, but I do

43

just wanna be with MiMi."

"Do you want to be with my son?"

I nodded my head and smiled.

"Well that's good," she said sitting back and lighting a cigarette. "I love my baby, he's all I got. All I ever wanted for him was a good woman. He doesn't need one to take care of him because I taught him how to take care of himself."

I nodded my head and smiled, but I couldn't help but feel envious. I wished I had a mother to take Kamden home to that would brag about all she'd taught me. Long ago I made myself say fuck having a mother, but at times like this, those suppressed feelings crept back.

"Kamden's punk ass father wasn't in his life like he should've been. I'm sure he told you that. Thankfully he had uncles in his life to teach him the things I couldn't."

Kamden nodded his head in agreement.

"Okay so let me shut up. Tell me about yourself MiMi. Did you grow up in Michigan?"

"Yes ma'am, in Beecher."

"I know Beecher. I used to be around that way sometimes."

"Yeah, I grew up on Peachtree. I lived with my father and big sister Shauna."

"What happened to your mother?"

"Um…she left to get milk for our cereal one morning and never came back."

Roxanne's face softened and she gave me a smile.

"I'm so sorry."

"It's okay."

44

"Well she missed out because you are a beautiful young woman."

There was an awkward silence, and Roxanne got up and went into the kitchen, her cigarette smoke following behind her.

"Let me get ya'll something to drink," she said over her shoulder.

Kamden pulled me closer to him and kissed me on the cheek.

"My momma likes you," he said laughing.

"She does? How do you know?"

"I can just tell. My Momma don't just give out compliments to anybody."

I smiled and felt relaxed for the first time since I'd gotten there. Although his mother was nothing like I expected, she was cool and I knew we would get along fine.

Kamden and I stayed at his mother's house for a few hours. She sent Kamden to get us something to eat and she and I spent the time getting to know each other. After we ate, Roxanne gave us both a hug before we left her house.

"It was so nice meeting you MiMi. Take good care of my son," she said to me as we embraced.

"I will. It was nice meeting you too."

Kamden and I left, and he drove me back to my apartment and parked in front.

"Did you have an okay time?" He asked.

"Yes, thanks for taking me to meet your mother."

He smiled and looked at me with a sexy look in his eyes.

"I wouldn't wanna take anybody else."

Taking off my seatbelt, I leaned over and kissed Kamden, sliding my tongue in his mouth.

"I love you," I said softly, almost hoping he didn't hear me.

"I love you too baby, I hope you can see that now."

Kamden bit my bottom lip, and I thought I was going to lose my mind.

"You want me to come in?" He asked.

"If you want to."

"You know I want to. I been wanting to do nasty things to you all day. You was so sexy at my Momma's house trying to be all innocent and polite."

I laughed and shook my head because the last thing I was thinking when I was at his Momma's house was trying to turn him on. Giving him one last peck on the lips I jumped out of the truck and dashed into my apartment with Kamden on my heels. I was wet and horny, and he was about to get it tonight. I was about to make sure he knew exactly how much I appreciated this change he was showing me.

CHAPTER 6

It was another day at work at the law firm; I was watching the clock like a hawk. My boss was at court and it was a slow day at the office. Since I was ahead on my work and it was almost time to go, I decided to text Kamden and see what he was up to. After waiting for a reply, he told me he was going to the gym to workout with his friends and that he would call me later. I straightened up my office before I locked up and left for the day. I hadn't even made it to my car before I got a call on my cell phone.

"Hello?"

"Naomi, you off work?" Shauna asked.

"Yeah, just got off. What's up?"

"I need a huge favor if you're not doing anything."

"What?"

"I'm held up at work and I got a doctor's appointment. Can you pick Jalil up from the babysitter and keep him for a few hours? I'll pick him up as soon as I leave the doctor's office."

"Yeah, I'll go get him right now. You okay?"

"Yeah, it's just I'm due for my annual pap smear."

"Oh yuck. Okay, well just call me when you get done, we should be at my apartment."

"Okay, thanks sissy."

"You know I got you."

"Auntie Nomi!" Jalil said, running to me when I walked into the daycare. His Team Oomizoomi backpack bounced on his back. He was dressed in blue jeans and a blue and white collared shirt. His hair was freshly cut in a fade and he had an earring in his ear.

"Hi big man! Did you miss me?"

"Yes, am I going with you?"

"Yes you are, go get all of your stuff."

Jalil gathered his toys and jacket as I talked to his babysitter. Shauna had already called and told her I would be coming to pick him up so she was informing me on his behavior that day.

"You know Jalil, he's just a ball of energy," the older black woman said. "You can't be mad at him. He's a growing boy."

I zipped up Jalil's jacket and we left the daycare with him telling me about school that day. I took him to get something to eat, then we went to the arcade and the toy store before we went back to my apartment. By the time I parked, Jalil was fast asleep in the backseat and I had to carry him in my apartment and put him in my bed. He'd only been sleep for about a half hour before Shauna called.

"What's my little man doing?"

"Sleeping, all played out."

"Where did you take him? You better not have been out spending all your money on him."

"What I spent on my nephew is none of your business."

Shauna laughed.

"Well I'm on my way to come get him."

"Okay, we're at my apartment."

Ten minutes later, Shauna was in my house and in my refrigerator getting whatever she could find to eat.

"You haven't been messing with the Sugar Daddy? He was giving you money all the time," she asked putting some of my takeout from lunch into the microwave. I laughed.

"His name is Joe, and no I do not mess around with him anymore. He keeps on calling me and leaving me messages and sending me flowers… I just don't respond. I do miss that money, but I told you me and Kamden's relationship is getting really serious. I'm only thinking about him."

"I'm proud of you Naomi, I think you and Kamden are going to have a beautiful relationship now. It seems like he's really grown up."

"He has. And you know his birthday is a few weeks before Thanksgiving so I wanna do something real special for him."

"Like?"

"I don't know, I haven't decided yet. I just want it to be different and fun for him."

"Well I'll put my thinking cap on."

Shauna sat at the counter island and I sat next to her.

"I met his Momma," I announced.

"You did? How was she?"

"She was nothing at all like I expected. She didn't have on a bra the whole time and was only wearing this little tank top! But she was cool, I liked her. Kamden said she liked me, but I don't know if he was just trying to make me feel good."

"She probably did. Everybody likes you Naomi. It's me that people have a hard time warming up to."

"Well thanks for the compliment," I said laughing. People did always think Shauna was mean. "I'm supposed to go meet some more of his family next week."

"Get the hell outta here! This is really getting serious!"

"Yes, I told you it was."

"So are you going to let him meet Daddy? When is the last time you talked to him anyway?"

"Not in a couple of months. You know me and Daddy's relationship is complicated."

Shauna gave me a disapproving look but didn't say anything else about it. We had always been close with our father, but my father and I had gotten into a big fight about a year before and nothing between us had been the same since.

"If things are getting serious and you're meeting his family, Daddy deserves to know. It's only right."

"Yeah, well if Daddy was interested in who was in my life and what was going on he knows my phone number and address."

Shauna dropped the issue and continued eating her food. The last time she tried to talk to me about my Daddy we ended up getting into an argument and didn't speak for a week. Throughout my life it always seemed Shauna was my father's favorite. Probably because the relationship between him and my mother was already on the rocks when she got pregnant with me and he had his doubts. When I grew up, all of that took a toll on my relationship with my father.

"So what are you and Jalil about to do?"

"Girl, go home and make him some dinner and try to relax. I am so exhausted, maybe he'll let me take a bubble bath tonight."

"Wait until he goes to sleep."

"When he goes to sleep I will have already have been sleep for three hours."

We laughed as Shauna cleaned up her mess, then went to go wake Jalil. He was still sprawled out on my bed with his mouth wide open like he had just gotten home from a twelve shift job.

"Jalil," Shauna sang. "Wake up baby, let's go home."

He stirred and tried to go back to sleep, but Shauna shook him some more and he finally opened his eyes.

"Come on, let's go home."

"I wanna stay with Auntie Nomi," he said and I smiled. I loved the way he pronounced my name.

"Auntie Nomi has things to do, and you have to go home and get a bath and eat dinner."

"I can do that here at Auntie Nomi's house." I couldn't help but laugh. He was too smart for his own good.

"Boy, get up. The decision is not up to you grown man. Let's go."

Jalil reluctantly got up and climbed off of my bed. I gave him a hug and a kiss before he put on his shoes and coat. I handed my sister the bags of toys I had gotten him from the store earlier.

"And you better not say nothing," I threatened. She looked in the bags and rolled her eyes.

"I don't know why you spoil him like this."

"Because he's my baby," I said holding out my hands to him. "Give me another hug and kiss big man."

Jalil smiled as he ran over to me and gave me a kiss as he wrapped his little arms around my neck.

"I love you Jalil, be good for Mommy."

"I will, love you Auntie Nomi."

I gave my sister a hug and a kiss before they left.

"Thank you so much Naomi. I'll call you later."

I locked the door behind my sister and nephew and watched them out the window until they got into the car and pulled away. Once I was alone, I pulled off all my clothes and lay on my couch with a throw blanket covering me. Jalil and Shauna weren't the only ones exhausted, and although it was still early, I watched TV on my couch until I fell asleep.

Hours later, I awoke to the ringing of my phone. It was dark in my apartment, except the glow from the television that was on with nobody watching. When I saw Kamden's name on the screen I answered quickly with a smile on my face.

"Hello?"

"Hey baby, you sleep?"

"Yeah. I had Jalil today and he wore me out."

Kamden laughed.

"Sorry I woke you up, I just wanted to ask you

something."

"What's up?"

"Well, since my Momma met you she hasn't stopped talking about you. My aunt wants to meet you, so I was gonna take you over there to meet her and my uncle. They practically helped my mother raise me-you see how crazy she is."

"So your aunt wants to meet me?" I asked, not hiding the happiness in my voice.

"Yeah, I told you my Momma likes you. I never brought anybody home before."

I smiled and breathed a sigh of relief. I was so worried Kamden's family wouldn't like me, but it seemed like so far I was off to a good start.

"I'm off Thursday."

"Cool, I'll take you by there then. So you miss me?"

"You know I do, are you coming to see me? I don't have any clothes on."

"Damn, I want to, but I can't tonight. Just send me a picture."

"Okay... What are you doing tonight?"

Kamden laughed.

"You always so suspicious. I'm going to visit my Uncle Amos. I been promising him I would come by and have a beer with him."

"Okay, well call me later. I might be up."

"I will. Dont forget to send me that picture."

"I won't."

CHAPTER 7

When Kamden and I pulled into his mother's driveway there was a silver Impala parked.

"That's my aunt's car," Kamden announced. I could tell he was excited. He talked about his Aunt Ginger and his Uncle Amos often; they were a big part of his life. Although I was nervous, the fact that I had already made a good impression on his mother made me relax a little. Things were happening so fast, but I was happy he was eager to introduce me to his family. I could definitely see the change in him.

Kamden led the way to the door and before he could knock it swung open. A short, heavyset woman was standing there wearing a brown sweater and blue jean pants.

"Nephew, hi!" She said to Kamden, but focused her attention on me. "You must be MiMi, nice to meet you."

I shook her hand.

"Yes ma'am, you must be his Aunt Ginger. It's a pleasure to finally meet you too. Kamden talks about you all the time."

"Kamden knows he better not bring a girl home unless she is up to my standards, that's why I'm so excited to finally meet you. You are adorable! She is cute Roxy!" she yelled over her shoulder. I laughed.

"Thank you."

We followed Ginger into the house which was much cleaner than before. There was a delicious smell that immediately hit me and my stomach instantly growled. Roxanne's home was completely different from the first time I had been there and I knew Ginger was the reason. Kamden explained to me that his mother had him when she was fifteen, and while she was a good mother, she refused to give up her life for her young son. That was where his Aunt Ginger and Uncle Amos stepped in. They provided him with a stable environment when his mother was running the streets.

Kamden's mother emerged from the kitchen wearing tight blue jeans and a cut up t-shirt. She was a nice looking woman for her age and had a nice body, but I could tell she was always happy to show it off.

"Baby," she sang as she wrapped her arms around Kamden. "You look handsome as always."

Next she gave me a hug.

"MiMi, it is so nice to see you again sweetie."

"Nice to see you too. Thank you for having me over again."

"Honey, you are welcome anytime, with or without Kamden. And I wanted you to meet my sister Ginger. She cooked tacos because Kamden knows I didn't cook a damn thing," she said laughing at her own joke.

"Well, let's eat before the meat gets cold," Ginger said leading the way into the kitchen. It was small, but bright and had mail piled up on the counters. On the table however, were all the fixings for good tacos and the meat was hot on the stove. We all sat down and after asking how many tacos everybody wanted, Ginger started to make the shells.

"So Naomi, tell me a little about yourself," Ginger said with her back to me as she moved around the stove gathering all of her ingredients.

"Well, I was born and raised in Beecher, graduated from Southwestern High School. I went to college at U of M for a couple years majoring in pre-law, but I didn't finish. I still want to go back though."

"Well it's never too late," Ginger said giving me an encouraging smile.

"Sis, fry my shells hard, you know I like mine crunchy," Roxanne said from where she was seated on the counter.

"I know Roxy, I've been making your tacos since you could eat them."

Roxanne laughed and continued scrolling through her phone.

"So what do your parents do for a living?"

"My father works for a construction company and my Mother hasn't been in my life since I was five years old."

"Right, Roxanne told me. I'm sorry to hear that."

"Thank you."

"You only have one sister?"

"Yeah, Shauna. She's five years older than me."

"Kam, you want your shells crunchy too, right?" Ginger asked pouring more grease into the skillet.

"Yes Ma'am."

"What about you MiMi?"

"I'll try mine crunchy too!"

"That's the best way to eat them," Ginger said winking at me.

"I got some daiquiri mix, we should've made drinks," Roxanne said, a smile spreading across her face. "You should never have Mexican food without liquor."

"You said that about Italian food," Ginger said laughing.

"And Chinese food," Kamden added. I couldn't help but laugh.

"I could use a Daiquiri right now," Ginger said. "Go ahead and go to the store and get some liquor Kamden."

Kamden sprung up from his seat and stretched.

"You wanna ride with me?" he asked me. Ginger objected before I had a chance to open my mouth.

"Take your Momma with you, you know she's the liquor expert."

"You don't have any objection from me on that," Roxanne said jumping off the counter.

"Get the money out of my purse Kamden."

"It's okay Auntie, I got it."

Ginger laughed and shook her head as Kamden followed his mother out of the kitchen.

"That boy never listens."

There was a moment of silence as Ginger busied herself at the stove and I looked through an Ebony magazine that had been sitting on the table.

"So MiMi, Roxanne has told me so much about you since she's met you. She was worried because Kamden was keeping her from you for so long," Ginger said turning briefly from the stove to look at me.

"Yeah, I don't know what that was about. I kept asking him to introduce me."

"Well you know how men are, they have to be ready to bring a woman home to Momma."

"Well I'm glad he finally came around. I really like Roxanne. She's hilarious!"

"That's Roxy. She's always been like that. Momma always said she could've sworn she came out of the womb laughing!"

Ginger and I both laughed.

"I really love being around Kamden and his Mom. The way she talks about him-I can tell she loves him so much. It does make me a little sad because I never had my mother in my life."

"Roxy mentioned that and I think that's horrible. I can't even imagine what your life was like without a mother and knowing she left the way she did."

"Yeah it was. Especially not knowing why she left us. I blamed my father for it and that caused a lot of problems between us. It still does."

It wasn't like me to open up to someone so easily but there was something about Ginger that made me feel like I could trust her. She seemed empathetic and sincere.

"Well if you don't mind my asking…was it something going on between the two of them that made you feel that way?"

I shrugged my shoulders.

"I don't really remember, I was so young. My sister was older but she never mentioned it. I just feel like he knows something he's not telling us. I mean, if there is something he knows don't you think he should tell us? We're her daughters."

"Yes, he should tell you. But MiMi, what if he really doesn't know? People do things unexpectedly sometimes for their own reasons. And even if they were going through something, that happens in relationships. I'm sure you know that. Me and my husband have definitely had our downs, but I never up and left."

Ginger paused for a minute and thought about what she had said.

"No disrespect to your mother at all, I just can't understand how a woman could do that to her children."

I shook my head to let her know I didn't take offense to her comment. Hell, anything negative anybody had to say about my mother I had already thought it anyway.

"When it's all said and done, I'm sure your father did everything he could to take care of you and your sister and that's what really matters. I'm sure he loved your mother and he went through his own pain when she left him to raise two girls alone. So try and cut him a little slack."

She said that last part like she was joking but I could tell she wasn't… and she was right. I had a lot of nerve blaming my father for any of my mother's actions after all he had done for me and Shauna. Talking to Ginger had definitely helped and I had a lot to think about when it came to the relationship I had with my father.

Ginger and I continued to talk and get to know each other while she finished preparing dinner. I learned that she had been married to Kamden's uncle Amos for thirty-eight years and they had one daughter, Francine. She lived in Delaware and had no children although Ginger had been praying for grandkids. Her husband worked as a truck driver which meant he spent a lot of time traveling and away from home. She was a nurse at Genesys Hospital and had been for the last twenty three years. By the time she was finishing up our tacos, we were laughing and talking like old friends and I felt as if I had known her forever.

"Hey! What's going on? It's too much laughter going on in here. Auntie, you aint sharing old embarrassing childhood stories of me are you?"

"Oh we were just getting to that nephew!" Ginger exclaimed still laughing at the joke I'd told her minutes earlier. "It took ya'll long enough. Did you have to drive to Mexico to get the tequila?"

"No," Roxanne said coming in carrying a bag of ice. "It doesn't matter because it's only going to take me a second to blend these drinks anyway. Ya'll know I'm a professional!"

We sat around the table and Ginger led us in grace before we all started to put our desired toppings on our tacos. When I bit into my first one, it tasted better than any other I had ever had in my life. I didn't know what I always did differently, but I had to learn Ginger's secret.

"Somebody has a birthday coming up," Roxanne sang munching on her taco. "What plans do you have baby?"

Kamden chewed his food before he answered.

"Well my girlfriend is probably going to be treating me to breakfast," Kamden said giving me a look. I laughed because we had never talked about this. "But other than that the fellas wanted to take me out later that night to be men and get drunk.

Ginger, Roxanne, and I all rolled our eyes and laughed. I didn't know what was amusing to them, but I figured it was because we were all thinking the same thing and it was nothing positive.

We talked, laughed, and enjoyed our food until it was almost ten. Ginger and Roxanne were so loving and so much fun and Kamden was blessed to have had two amazing women in his life. Ginger and Roxanne both hugged and kissed me and Kamden before we left the house. They made sure to invite me to Thanksgiving dinner and I told them I wouldn't miss it for the world. So far it seemed my relationship with Kamden was progressing wonderfully and I was earning extra brownie points if his family's feelings had anything to do with it.

CHAPTER 8

Being in a relationship had its perks, but there were some things I missed about being single. Kamden had a job and also went to school, so he wasn't always available to me like I wanted him to be. I missed the days when I had a list of men I could call for whatever I wanted. However, my love for Kamden outweighed my need for attention. The only man I wanted was him and when he wasn't available, I found other things to occupy my time. My latest was yoga class. I went every Monday and Wednesday after work and it was only right that I took my best friend along with me. Kapri loved working out, and she jumped at the opportunity to stretch her muscles. We carried our yoga mats into the building and waited patiently, sipping water and eating cheese crackers before our class started.

"So, how have things been between you and your dude?"

"Things are going great between me and Kamden," I said laughing. "Why do you hate him so much?"

"I am not going to answer that question because I cannot

do so without bashing him. If he is making you happy, then that's good. Maybe he's changing… finally."

"He is. I met his Mom and Aunt."

"And how did that go?"

"It actually went well. I met his Mom first and she really like me, so she wanted me to meet his Aunt. She made us tacos and they invited me over for Thanksgiving."

"Are you going?"

"Of course I am. I want to meet his family. His Mom and Aunt were really nice, so hopefully everybody else is too."

"They will be- everybody likes you."

"I don't know why everybody says that," I said laughing. "How are things with you and Brock?"

"Things are good. I'm trying to take it slow, but the sex is so fucking good I would marry him tomorrow if he asked me."

"Kapri, you are crazy," I laughed.

"Well, it's true. I am starting to feel so free sexually and he is opening me up to so many different things I never tried before."

"Like what?"

"Public sex," she whispered and bit her cracker with a smirk on her face.

"Public? Like where?"

"I mean, we don't just go in the middle of the street in broad daylight and start having sex… but sometimes we go in the bathroom at restaurants and bookstores. Oh, once we went to the library and had sex and we had to be discrete and quiet. It was hot."

I nodded my head, but in my mind my wheels were spinning. I got most of my crazy sex ideas from Kapri and this time was no different. It was about time I added some new stuff for Kamden in the bedroom.

"So are you and Brock dating exclusively?"

"I'm not sure. I think he's been talking to other girls so I still have friends, but I've only been having sex with him... and the way he works it, I don't need anybody else," Kapri said with a sly smile. "I mean girl, I have never had anything like it."

"I'm glad you found somebody. I haven't had a chance to talk to him as much as I would like, but I think he's nice."

"He is. And he treats me so good. You know, it's one of those things where it's kind of too good to be true, and that's what's scary."

I didn't have a chance to respond because our yoga instructor opened the door and we went inside to start our meditation. I was genuinely happy Kapri had a man, I just hoped she was enjoying it and not waiting for the other shoe to fall.

That evening Kamden came over with dinner. I was wearing next to nothing; a cute satin black and yellow pajama set and I made sure my apartment was clean and smelling like strawberries. When he came carrying the brown paper bags stuffed with Cantonese cuisine and the bottle of red wine, I kissed him on the lips and went into the kitchen to grab the wine glasses.

"Did you miss me?" I asked when I came back into the

living room carrying the goblets.

"You know I did. How was work?" he asked, sitting on the couch and taking the food out of the bags.

"It was cool. Then I went to my yoga class with Kapri."

Kamden laughed.

"My worst enemy. She still hate me?"

"As much as she did the last time you asked. What did you do to my best friend?"

"I don't know why she doesn't like me. That's your friend, you never asked her?"

"Yeah, and she never told me the reason."

"That must mean she doesn't have one," Kamden said pulling me on top of him and giving me another kiss. "Now, did you miss me?"

"You know I did baby."

We sat on the couch kissing like two horny teenagers before we remembered we had food that was getting cold. After filling our paper plates with fried chicken, broccoli beef, chow mein noodles, and egg rolls we sat and talked while we enjoyed our meal. Although Kamden and I had been together for years, it seemed lately we were really getting to know each other. We hadn't talked that intimately in so long, yet I was starting to feel more confident that we were going to make it. I could see Kamden was making an effort to change and that made me want to do something special for him. With his birthday right around the corner, I decided to try and pick his brain and find out what he wanted.

"So you told your Mom and Aunt that you wanted me to take you to breakfast, what was that about?" I asked.

"I like pancakes," he answered shrugging his shoulders.

"I know you like pancakes," I laughed, "but you never mentioned anything to me about wanting to go to breakfast for your birthday."

"Well, my Uncle is going to take me to lunch, and then that night my boys wanna take me out."

"So you're just gonna squeeze me in when you have a hole in your schedule basically?"

"Well, everybody else already told me what they wanted to do. I didn't think you was tryna be with me on my birthday."

"Don't be stupid. Of course I wanna be with you on your birthday," I said as he refilled my wine glass.

"Well you didn't say anything baby, that's why I said breakfast… and maybe we can do something before I go out with the boys."

I nodded my head, but didn't say anything. It was clear Kamden didn't have time for me on his birthday and I wasn't going to force my way in. If he wanted time with me on his birthday he would've have made time and not filled up his day with everybody else.

"What's wrong MiMi? You mad at me?"

I shook my head and continued to eat my food without making eye contact with him. I didn't want to seem selfish because it was *his* birthday, but my feelings were hurt. I knew I was overreacting and I didn't want him to see that.

"Yes you are. Baby, I'm sorry. You know I didn't do it on purpose."

"Kamden, it's cool. We'll go to Ihop first thing in the morning on your birthday that way we can get it out the way."

Kamden put his fork down and leaned over.

"Give me a kiss and quit trippin'."

I leaned over to give him a quick peck to shut him up, but he grabbed the back of my head and stuck his tongue into my mouth giving me no choice but to sit there and be kissed. I hated him but loved him at the same time, and after our lips parted I was all smiles and forgot all about being mad. This was the reason I wanted a life with Kamden, because with him it was impossible to be mad and not have a smile on my face.

CHAPTER 9

"Hi ya'll, I'm so happy ya'll are here!" Tarissa said as she opened the door to her brand new apartment. She had been missing in action for months, but I didn't blame her because she was working her ass off to stack her chips and get her own place. Now she had settled into a one bedroom apartment in Davison, right down the street from the high school. It was a nice neighborhood, and now that she was all moved in, she wanted to have a housewarming party to celebrate.

"Of course we're here!" Shauna said, handing her a wrapped gift. "Congratulations on your new place!"

"Thank you," she said hugging Shauna.

"Congratulations boo!" I said hugging her and giving her a fifth of tequila. "You know I think liquor is more of a gift for a new apartment. You'll need a few shots once those bills start rolling in."

"Aint that the truth," Tarrissa said gladly accepting the bottle. "Well let me show you around," she said leading us in to her kitchen first to drop off the wine and tequila. It was a medium-sized kitchen with wooden cabinets and marble countertops. The floor was hard wood and she had crème carpet. Her living room was spacious and had a big bay window which complimented her orange and black couch and love seat and black rug. Tarrissa had done such a good job decorating that I was tempted to ask her to redecorate my apartment!

"I'll show you both my room when everybody leaves. You know I like my privacy," she whispered.

"Is your girl coming?" I asked, leading the way into the kitchen so Shauna and I could indulge in the appetizers Tarrissa had made.

"She said she was coming when she got off of work."

"And everything is going well between the two of you?" Shauna asked.

"So far so good," Tarrissa said with a bright smile. "She stays over here sometimes and I still go to her place now and then. We're good."

"Well I'm glad, and I hope it works out between you and Sabrina because I know you really love her."

We joined the party and mingled with all of the guests. Since the three of us were so close we knew all of her friends and were already comfortable with everybody. Alex, one of Tarrissa's guy friends who had a crush on Shauna was there, so she cozied into a corner with him. I sat on the loveseat with Tarrissa's best friend Haley. She was a Mexican girl with long black hair and hazel almond shaped eyes. Laughing was non-stop when I was sitting next to her because she was a comedian and liked to talk and joke about everything. Seeing

Haley at a party meant that you would literally leave in stitches because she was that damn funny.

"I can't believe Riss is still friends with Janet from high school," Haley said shaking her head with a serious look on her face. She pointed at the chocolate beauty with long braids that she wore up in a bun. She did have a really big booty and a nice physique, but I wasn't into chicks.

"She had to wear kneepads when she walked across the graduation stage because she spent her whole four years on them."

"Haley," I said trying my best not to crack up laughing.

"I'm serious. It's a shame too because I was gonna let her lick it," Haley said biting her lips. She was openly bisexual and had no problem expressing her interest about whomever.

"Well, that was a long time ago-maybe she changed."

Haley shrugged her shoulders as I scanned the apartment looking for my cousin but she was nowhere in sight.

"I'll be right back," I told Haley getting up from where I was seated on the couch.

I went through the apartment in search of Tarrissa, but I couldn't find her anywhere. It was unlike Tarrissa to leave any party especially her own, so I knew she was up to something. After opening the door to her bedroom and knocking on the bathroom door I was just about ready to give up when I heard whispering coming from a door at the very end of the hallway. I knocked lightly, and when I opened it, my mouth fell open. Tarrissa was pinned in the corner with her hands over her head, and she was being tongued down and felt up by some chick with short hair and tattoos. I was confused because the last thing Tarrissa had said to me was how happy she was with her girlfriend, but I didn't say anything. Quietly, I closed the door and went back in the living room to the party. Tarrissa had a lot of explaining to do.

Back in the living room, my seat had been taken, but when I saw the person sitting there I couldn't even be mad. Janet, the girl Haley had just been telling me about, was seated in my old seat next to Haley, who was running her fingers through her own hair and looking at Janet as if she was interested in whatever she had to say. When she noticed me she smiled and gave me a wink and I couldn't help but laugh. Shauna was still with Alex looking all too comfortable and it was only then that I realized I was the odd girl out. Pouring myself another drink, I sat in a barstool in the corner and scrolled through my phone while watching everyone else. Before long there was a knock at the door and Sabrina entered scanning the room obviously looking for Tarrissa. I went and intercepted before my cousin got caught up.

"Hey girl!" I said hugging her as if we were old friends. "I heard you were coming. Rissa was all excited about it."

"Aww," she said flashing me a smile. "I tried to get the day off work, but they weren't letting that happen."

"I know how it is. I never get a day off that I want. Especially because I'm the best at what I do."

We laughed and I looked around the room for Tarrissa who was still not in the room. I kept Sabrina entertained with a drink and small talk while I waited for my cousin to emerge from the closet. Once I realized that wasn't happening soon enough, I got Shauna's attention and mouthed for her to go find Rissa.

After chatting with Sabrina for far too long about work, music, yoga and any other topic I could come up with, Tarrissa finally emerged with a huge smile on her face.

"Hey baby, how was work?" Tarrissa said giving Sabrina the same kiss I'd just seen her giving tattooed chick ten minutes earlier.

"It was good, but I couldn't wait to get off and see you," she said kissing Tarrissa again on the lips. "You look so sexy."

"Thanks babe, now come here," Tarrissa said grabbing her hand. "I wanna introduce you to some people you haven't met yet."

They went across the living room and started talking to some of Tarrissa's high school friends. Tattoo chick discreetly came out of the living room closet and into the kitchen to fix herself a drink. If I didn't know Tarrissa was a player before that night, there was definitely no doubt in my mind now. I had to laugh because there was so much happening at this small housewarming. Shaking my head and chuckling, I went back to my seat in the corner, charged my phone and watched the entire night play out.

Once the party was over, Shauna and I stayed to help Tarrissa clean up. Sabrina had went to take a shower and was making plans to take Tarrissa out to the bar for a late date. I used the opportunity to drill Riss about what I had walked in on.

"Sooooo," I said giving her a look before I went on. "What is going on with that girl?"

"What girl?" Shauna asked loudly, defeating the purpose

of my whisper.

"Shh!"

"Oh, you mean Randi?" Riss said with a giggle.

"If you're talking about the girl you were in the closet with, that's exactly who I mean."

"Well I will tell you about her later," Riss said looking towards the bathroom. "But just know she wants me bad and has for a very long time. She was pissed when I got into a relationship."

"Yeah, well you make sure you call me and tell me about that because I am very interested to know who she is and why I haven't met her," I whispered one more time before changing the subject. "Your housewarming was fun. Only you could have a housewarming with so many people everywhere. How do you make so many friends?"

"Everybody likes me! I can't help it! It's a gift and a curse."

We stayed and kept Riss company until Sabrina got ready. We all walked out together and I got into the passenger seat of Shauna's car. She'd picked me up from my apartment since I lived on the way to Riss's new place.

"So, who is the girl you and Riss were talking about? You know I couldn't wait to ask."

"Girl! So I was looking for her to ask her something and for some reason I opened her hall closet, and there she was getting slobbed down by some chick with tattoos. I mean *slobbing*, hands all over her head and everything. Where was she when I told you to go find her?"

"In her bedroom. She looked like she had been caught with her hands in the cookie jar!" Shauna exclaimed laughing as she pulled out of the apartment complex.

"Yup, right before her girlfriend got there. I thought she was caught up!"

Shauna shook her head and continued to laugh.

"I knew Riss was a player! She said Sabrina ain't gonna break her heart no more!"

"I'm telling you, that's how you gotta be sometimes. Why put all your eggs in one basket when you don't know if that person is going to be faithful?"

"So what about you? Are you still spreading your eggs around while you're with Kamden?"

"Me? No, I'm actually being faithful this time. He's serious and I want it to work."

"Aww, I'm proud of you Naomi, you're growing up. I might be a maid of honor sooner than I thought."

"Maybe. His Mom and Aunt really like me, I'm going to meet the rest of his family on Thanksgiving."

"When are you going to let him meet Daddy?"

"Shauna, don't go there," I warned.

She didn't say anything for a minute, so I decided to break the awkward silence.

"So, while you're trying to keep me focused on Rissa's messiness, what was going on with you and Alex hugged up in the corner all night?"

"We were just talking," she said blushing, making it known there was a little more to it than that. "He's always been really nice...young, but nice. I'm thinking about giving him some, but then you know how that goes, I'll never be rid of him. Look at my baby daddy."

I laughed and we continued to talk about the party and all the craziness that went on until we pulled up to my apartment. Shauna and I both had to work the next morning so she didn't come in; we just hugged and professed our sisterly love to one another before I went inside and got ready for bed.

CHAPTER 10

"Do you feel older yet?" I asked eyeballing Kamden from the driver's seat of his Durango. It was his birthday and I was on my way to take him to get his pancakes like he'd asked.

"Nah, still feel the same age. Maybe in a couple hours, it's still early."

Kamden put his hand on my thigh as we cruised down the street with the music on low. I kept stealing glances at him because he looked so damn sexy. His hair was freshly cut, thanks to a visit the previous day to his barber, Money. His gray button up jacket was open revealing the Polo shirt I'd bought him for his birthday. The light blue jeans he was wearing matched perfectly with his shirt, and he set it all off with a crispy pair of blue and white Nike's.

"You keep on peekin' over here I'm gonna give you something to look at."

"You already are. You look good baby, that shirt looks nice on you."

"Thanks, you got good taste babe," he said, scrolling

through his phone. He started smiling at something, and then put it back into his jacket pocket.

"What are you so happy about?"

"What? Nothing," he said squeezing my thigh and blowing me a kiss. "Quit being nosey."

"Um hum, quit being sneaky."

"Baby, don't start that. You can trust me, I'm not gonna fuck up this time. I'm gonna marry you."

"We'll see. You better act right."

"I got you again don't I? You know I ain't going nowhere."

As soon as I stopped at a red light I leaned over and gave Kamden a kiss because it was his birthday and because I was so happy we were finally in a good place in our relationship. I was extremely happy with him and the way things were going, so he was right. I needed to put my insecurities away and enjoy being happy with the man I loved.

When we arrived at Ihop we were seated in a booth that faced the busy street. I looked over my menu and decided on what I wanted as the waiter took our drink order.

"So where are the boys taking you tonight?"

"I don't know, you know they always last minute at everything. They actin' like they gonna do it all big for me, but we'll probably just end up at some strip club. Them niggas use any excuse to see some tits and ass."

It took everything inside of me to not make a smart comment. I wasn't a very big fan of Kamden's friends and they weren't very big fans of me. Whenever Kamden hung around them it seemed trouble wasn't too far behind. I couldn't blame his friends for his past actions though; he was a grown man and had to be accountable for his own actions.

"This is the highlight of my birthday anyway, breakfast with you," he said grabbing my hand.

"Yeah, it better be," I said smiling and flipping the page on my menu.

"MiMi, I have a question," Kamden said seriously.

"Okay," I said dropping my menu and giving him my undivided attention.

"You already met my Momma and my Auntie, and they both love you. You're going to meet the rest of my family on Thanksgiving… so when are you going to introduce me to your family?"

"You've met Shauna and Tarrissa."

"I mean your father MiMi."

"My relationship with my father is complicated right now baby."

"I know, we talked about that MiMi, but that won't last forever. I'm planning on taking this relationship to new levels and as a man I don't wanna do that without your father's blessing."

I understand that and I appreciate it." Thankfully the waiter came to take our order so I didn't have to answer right away. "I'll work on things with my Daddy and then once we're better I'll introduce you to him."

Kamden smiled that smile that always could melt my heart and make me do anything he wanted me to. Being with him was what I thought love was supposed to feel like and I never wanted it to go away. If Kamden meeting my father was the only thing holding us back from taking the relationship further that was something I had to plan to work on.

Sitting back in the booth, I watched as Kamden finished the last of his pancakes. Thanks to my hearty appetite I had already devoured my stack of blueberry pancakes and sausage links so I sat there too full to move and pay the bill that lay face down on the table.

"Did you enjoy your pancakes honey?"

Kamden nodded his head with a big smile and a mouthful of cinnamon pancakes. He looked extremely happy and that was enough to make me happily pay the bill and leave a nice tip for my man's birthday breakfast.

We listened to one of Kamden's rap cd's as I drove back to my apartment. Kamden's phone was blowing up; friends and relatives were calling to wish him a happy birthday. Most calls he answered, others he ignored. When we made it to my house, he got out and gave me a hug and kiss before he got into the driver's seat.

"I love you baby. Thank you for breakfast," he said wrapping his arms around my waist and resting his hands on the top of my butt.

"You're welcome baby. Happy birthday and I love you too!"

Kamden got into his car as I sashayed into my apartment and giving Kamden a little show because as always, I knew he was watching. He waited until I was safely inside before he took off. I went into my apartment and waited a few minutes before I left out again. I knew Kamden would be busy all day with his friends and family celebrating his birthday and I would be getting my surprise ready for when he got home from the club.

I sat in the parking lot of Lover's Lane waiting for Tarrissa to help me pick out lingerie and sex games for Kamden and I to enjoy that night. Not only was Tarrissa the freakiest person I knew, she hadn't called me to explain about the tattooed chick I'd caught her with in the closet. When she pulled up I got out of my car and hugged her.

"Riss! Hi baby, thanks for meeting me."

"No problem I'm glad you called me."

Tarrissa followed me into the store and we were greeted by the salesperson. We declined her help and browsed the store on our own.

"Why did you come to Lover's Lane? Isn't this store for old people?" Tarrissa said looking through the lingerie.

"Lover's Lane is for all ages, I thought this is where everybody came."

"Not me, but we'll see what they have."

"So," I said picking up a purple dildo that was on display and turning it on. "You know I didn't have you meet me out here just to help me pick out sex stuff."

"What else did you have me meet you for Naomi?"

"Because you never called to tell about tattoo chick you were slobbing down in the closet at your party."

Tarrissa laughed and her whole face instantly lit up.

"Randi and I met at Beerfest last summer. She followed

me around the whole night and we were flirting with each other and she asked me for my number. We continued to mess around that entire summer and into the fall until me and Sabrina got back together. She was pissed when I told her too and she makes it clear every time she sees me."

I continued to explore the dildos as I listened to the love story of Randi and Tarrissa.

"When she took me in the closet she knew Sabrina was about to be there, that's why she did it. It's a turn on for her to see me with my girlfriend knowing she just did things with me in the closet. She was sending me freaky texts all night."

Tarrissa had a look in her eye when she talked about Randi that she didn't have with Sabrina. I wasn't going to mention it unless she asked me though.

"Ooh, do you want Ben Wa Balls?" She asked, picking up a blue box.

"Are those the metal balls you put inside yourself?"

Tarrissa nodded her head.

"No thank you. What if they get stuck inside me?"

"They won't. And if something happens and you can't get them out you just lie down and go to sleep and when you wake up they'll be out of you."

"Yeah, because I'll be able to go to sleep when I have metal balls stuck inside me."

We both laughed as she put the box back on the shelf and continued our browsing. They had everything from whips, chains and nipple clamps, to edible panties and body paint. I found some games and toys I thought Kamden would enjoy before we made our way to the lingerie section. I sifted through the racks trying to find something that would be flattering to my physique.

"Everything is fucking ugly," Tarrissa said with her nose turned up. "I don't see anything that would look good on you."

"That's because you're not looking," I said holding up a sexy police officer lingerie set. "I can arrest him for being a bad boy."

"Role playing," Tarrissa said. " Not my thing, but if that's what ya'll like that's cool. You'll look sexy in that."

I put the lingerie set over my arm and continued browsing. By the time we had gone through all the racks I had the police set, a red and white nurse's uniform, and a hot pink and black set with a see through top and thong underwear. After looking back and forth between the three sets I chose the nurse uniform and put the other two back. I was excited as the cashier rang me up. I knew Kamden and I would have fun that night and that he would be speechless about the things I had up my sleeve. I couldn't wait!

"So, you know you can no longer call me a freak right?" Tarrissa said as we walked out of the store.

"Why not? You are a freak."

"After the things I found out about you today, you are not too far behind me."

I didn't try to object because she was probably right about that. I was getting older and learning more and more about my sexuality and having so much fun. The best part about it was I was doing it all with the man I loved... hopefully the man that would one day be my husband.

"Well you'll have to let me know how tonight goes and how Kamden likes his gifts," she said as she got into her car.

"I will. And don't think you're off the hook because I got distracted today. I want to hear more about this Randi girl."

Tarrissa blushed a little and then started her engine. I headed back to my apartment to count down the hours until I could give my man the real birthday surprise I had planned.

The hours seemed to drag by as I tried to keep myself distracted and not looking at the clock until I went to Kamden's house. I planned to already be near his house when he got in from the club, and be knocking at the door as soon as he closed it for the night. Once he saw me standing there in my black trench coat and let me in, I would drop it and reveal my nurse outfit and red pumps. I would be his naughty nurse for the night and it would be my job to fulfill all of his freaky fantasies. I would be carrying a duffel bag full of toys and games and we would make use of them all night and into the morning. I replayed the scene over again in my head as I got out of the shower, oiled up and perfumed in preparation for my trip to Kamden's. After putting all of my Lover's Lane purchases in a black duffel bag, I turned off the lights before I left my apartment.

When I pulled up to Kamden's house, the hairs on the back of my neck immediately started to stand because I knew something wasn't right. Kamden's car was in the driveway right behind a silver Lexus that I didn't recognize. Instead of parking down the street like I had originally planned, I pulled up behind the Lexus, left my duffel bag in the car, and walked straight to the door. My black trench coat slapped against my calves, and my abrupt knock on the door replaced my heartbeat as I waited for a response. I could hear slow music, the kind my daddy called "baby making music" playing from inside the house, and when the door opened, I tried to keep my mouth from hitting the floor. Standing in front of me was Rebecca, the girl Kamden had been in a relationship with the first year of his relationship with me. She was wearing only Kamden's blue and black robe. Giving me a sly smile, she stood before me with her arms crossed. I didn't say a word, just stood there near tears because this woman had once again achieved at stealing my happiness.

CHAPTER 11

"MiMi," Rebecca said with a smirk. It seemed I was always in competition with her, but this time I had truly thought she was out of the picture. She flipped her long black hair over her shoulder.

"Kamden can't come to the door right now...he's a little... preoccupied."

She smiled again, this time showing all of her perfect white teeth and making her green eyes disappear. I wanted to smack the shit out of her. I had always thought I was damn fine, but Rebecca was beautiful. She was the only female that could make me feel insecure about myself. It was something about her that Kamden couldn't stay away from and I couldn't help but wonder what she had that I didn't.

"What are you doing here?" I asked, only because I didn't know what else to say.

"I couldn't let my baby's birthday pass without coming to properly wish him a happy one...mission accomplished."

Rebecca gave me another slick ass smile and before I knew it I had pushed her into the wall and went into the house to find Kamden. He was coming out of the bathroom wearing only his underwear. Before he realized who was standing in front of him, I was already slapping the shocked look off of his stupid ass face.

"Really Kamden?! Fa real?? You been playing me all this time!"

Kamden was trying to come towards me to respond, but I just kept swinging. I was hurt, humiliated, and heartbroken. Kamden had deceived me once again and I was looking like a damn fool. No other man had ever been able to manipulate my mind the way he did and have me second guessing what I already knew: Kamden was a cheater and that was never going to change.

"MiMi, listen, please baby. I'm so sorry. Just let me explain what's going on."

"Kamden you don't have anything else to explain because I am done with you. Don't ever call me again or come to my apartment because you and that dirty bitch deserve each other!" I screamed at him making sure I was loud enough for him to hear me before I left the house. I wasn't about to give him the satisfaction of seeing tears fall down my face. He had already humiliated me enough, I wasn't about to look like a fool crying in front of Rebecca...she would get too much satisfaction out of that. I hopped into my car and burned rubber as I pulled out of his driveway. He was chasing behind me so close that I tried to run over his fucking feet. I watched him in my rearview mirror standing in the middle of the street in his underwear with his hands on his head. It wasn't until then that I started crying like a baby. It was a pain that came deep from my soul and I couldn't stop the tears. I waited until I was at a red light before I pulled out my phone and called my sister.

"Hello?"

"Shauna, I'm so... so fucking pissed!"

"Naomi, what's wrong?"

"Kamden is cheating... he's cheating on me!" I cried. I could barely talk because I was sobbing profusely and my adrenaline was high.

"Okay, Naomi calm down. Try to calm down and come to my house."

"Okay."

"You wanna stay on the phone until you get here?"

"No, I think I'll be okay," I said trying to take deep breaths. "I'm just gonna turn on some music until I get there."

"I'm not getting off the phone until you stop crying."

Shauna waited a few minutes until I calmed myself down and we got off of the phone. I turned up the radio and let the tears fall silently as the music filled my car.

"I can't believe I ever thought he would change, "I said as Shauna poured me another shot of vodka. I was sitting at her kitchen table with her wearing a pair of her sweatpants and a t-shirt. My face was a mess and my eyes were puffy and red. It was humiliating to have to show up at my sister's door only wearing a lingerie set, red heels and a trench coat, but my sister was there for me without being judgmental. She just gave me some pajamas and poured me a drink. I downed the shot as quickly as I could and motioned for her to pour me another one. My phone was turned off and on the charger because Kamden wouldn't stop calling me and since I refused to answer, turning it off was the only way to keep my sanity.

"I am just in shock. I was rooting so hard for him too. Asshole," Shauna said taking a shot of her own.

"I just don't understand what it is about her that I don't have. No matter what I do, he can't seem to leave her alone."

"It doesn't have anything to do with you. He's a man and that's what they do. Just go back to doing you and have fun. Don't let him sweet talk you either, keep ignoring his calls."

"If he keeps calling me like he has been I won't even be able to turn my phone on."

"Change your number."

I took another shot and held my breath until the taste was gone.

"You should slow down Naomi. You're staying here tonight."

"That was the plan. I can't go back to my place, he'll just show up. He's probably sitting outside my apartment right now. I just wanna get drunk until I don't even remember his name."

Shauna didn't say another word, just smiled and poured us another shot. I didn't want to keep crying, but I could feel the tears coming again. Every time I thought about Rebecca standing in the door smiling at me like she had one up on me, and Kamden being half-naked, I got sick to my stomach. In the past I'd forgiven Kamden for a lot of things, but this was something I didn't see myself ever getting over.

When I woke up early the next morning I was in my nephew's twin bed with a Ninja Turtles comforter over my body. I had cried and drunk so much alcohol the night before that I had a blackout. I didn't remember what had happened and it took me a minute to figure out why I was here, at Shauna's. Once I did, my heart got heavy again, but I refused to give Kamden another second of my happiness.

I stumbled as quietly as I could through the house looking for my phone. It was powered off and on the charger where I'd left it. After grabbing it, I turned it on, and sat on the couch to stop the room from spinning. I immediately started getting alerts: 63 missed calls, 23 text messages, 11 voicemails... and I knew most of them were from Kamden. Since I didn't feel like hearing his voice, I decided to read the text messages.

After going through them and deleting our message history I laid down on the couch and closed my eyes. I had a splitting headache and I couldn't stop the room from spinning. I figured a few more hours of sleep would help me get rid of this hangover. I awoke not too long afterwards to someone poking me.

"Auntie Nomi," he whispered, still poking me on my forehead.

"What Jalil?" I asked, finally opening my eyes. I was hoping he would go away, but he was going to continue to poke me until I got up.

"Do you know where my Momma is?"

I finally sat up and looked around. The last time I

remembered Shauna was there. I got up and Jalil followed me around the apartment only to find out Shauna was, in fact, gone. I immediately called her cell phone.

"Hello?" She answered sounding upbeat.

"Hey, where did you go?"

"I woke you up and told you I was going to get some breakfast, remember?"

"No."

"Well you were asleep in Jalil's bed, but when I got ready to leave you were on the couch. I woke you up and told you I was going to get us something to eat."

"Well I don't remember. Jalil just woke me up and asked me where you were."

"I'm on my way back. I'll be there in about five minutes."

"Okay."

I hung up the phone and smiled at my nephew.

"Your Momma went to get us some food. She'll be here in a minute. You wanna watch cartoons?"

Jalil nodded his head and I turned the TV on a show he told me was called *Phineas and Ferb*. He made sure to narrate exactly what was going on so that I was paying attention. I was relieved when Shauna walked in, already dressed in jeans and a t-shirt underneath her jacket. She was carrying three bags of styrofoam takeout boxes. Jalil and I both followed her in the kichen and when she opened the boxes we saw she had purchased a variety of breakfast foods. I made Jalil and I both a plate and sat at the table. After having breakfast with them, I decided it was time to face reality and head home.

CHAPTER 12

"Why the fuck are you at my door?" I asked leaving the chain lock on my door so it would only open an inch. Kamden stood there with his hands in his jacket pocket. He had continued to blow my phone up constantly, but I never picked up. Since I refused to change my number as Shauna had suggested, I just blocked his and tried to move on with my life. I thought he had gotten the hint until now.

"MiMi-"

"Don't fucking call me that, I'm not gonna tell you again."

Kamden paused for a minute like he didn't know what to say.

"Can I please come in?" He asked softly, his voice trembling. "I just wanna talk to you for a minute."

"Then talk."

"What happened the other night with Rebecca did not mean anything to me. I didn't know she was coming to town, she just showed up at my door."

I immediately shook my head.

"You and I celebrated your birthday early because you told

me you were spending the evening with your friends. I show up at your house at the time the clubs are supposed to let out and you're already home with Rebecca? What did you do, cancel with your friends, or leave early?"

"I had already left when she showed up."

"So she just conveniently knew you would be home?"

Kamden started looking like he didn't know what to say and for me the conversation was just like our relationship... over. I shut the door in his face and locked it before he had a chance to answer my question. He and I both knew what had happened that night; he didn't need to make up fairy tales to try to save my feelings.

"Baby, please don't do this. I love you, I don't give a damn about that bitch. You are the one I wanna spend the rest of my life with," he said from the other side of the door. Tears started to sting my eyes because I did love Kamden, and I knew not opening that door was giving him the opportunity to run to Rebecca and that thought killed me. However, as hard as it was, I did not let myself open the door and after awhile he gave up and left. Dialing Kapri's number, I got a carton of ice cream out of the refrigerator and went into my bedroom.

"Hello?"

"So guess who just showed up at my door?"

"Who Kamden? Yuck. What the hell did he want?"

"To talk, apologize, tell me she didn't mean anything to him."

"So you let him in?"

"Hell no. I left the chain on the damn door and cracked it.

He wasn't about to come in here and sweet talk me out of my panties."

"Yup, because that's exactly what he would've did. I'm proud of you baby, I know that was hard. I know you still love him."

"I do, but I deserve better. I wanna just move on and have fun. I'm not trying to have a relationship."

"Well speaking of fun, how do you feel about a weekend in Miami?"

"That sounds nice, but I don't know if my bank account thinks so."

"Well, this sounds like a nice time to mend fences with Daddy. You know he'll help you foot the bill."

"Girl, I don't know about that one. I haven't talked to my Daddy in months."

"Well now is the perfect time to call him crying about the breakup. You need a vacation anyway."

"What's in Miami?"

"Well Brock was taking me and he told me his cousin was asking if you were interested in going."

"Well if he wants to know if I'm interested why the hell am I worrying about how to pay?"

"That's a question you should be asking him. Want his number?"

"No, but you can give him mine."

"Okay," Kapri said sounding excited. "I'll tell Brock to have him call you asap."

I hung up and continued eating my ice cream. Before long my phone was ringing.

"What's up pretty lady. I'm glad you changed your mind and let me call you."

As soon as I heard his voice I smiled because it was nice to hear.

"Thank you. I'm glad I changed my mind as well."

"I could tell last time you didn't want to give me your number."

"I know, I'm sorry. I was still dealing with my ex and I didn't want to give you any false hope in case we got back together… which we did."

"And how is that going?"

"It's not going…we broke up."

"That's fucked up, sorry to hear that," he said, but I could tell he wasn't sorry at all. If Kamden and I hadn't broken up I wouldn't be on the phone with him and he knew that.

"Thanks for saying that even though I know you don't mean it."

"I do. I mean, I am sorry because I know you're hurting, and a beautiful woman should never be hurting because of a man. But obviously I'm glad I'm talking to you now. I hope I can see you soon so I can make you smile again."

Everything Rashad was saying I had heard before, but at this point I was vulnerable and I needed a man… preferably between my legs. Since Rashad was cool and talking, I thought why not see what he was all about. I didn't know if the Miami trip was going to happen, but if it did Rashad had better been bringing some good dick along with him if he ever thought he was going to keep my attention.

"When are you trying to see me?"

"As soon as I can."

"What if I told you I wanted to see you tonight, what would you say?"

"I would be telling you when and where to meet me."

"Oh, you're telling me?" I asked liking Rashad a little more. This demanding attitude he was giving me was quite a turn-on.

"Oh yeah. Once you show me interest, I don't wait for directions. Boys wait, men take action and I'm a man all day long baby."

"You talkin' good, the question is can you back up all those words."

"Wait until tonight is over and you can be your own witness."

Rashad gave me directions on where to meet him before we got off of the phone. I finished my ice cream before I got ready to get in the bathtub. I'd always heard the best way to get over a new man was to get under a new one and since eating ice cream and watching TV wasn't working, I figured it was time to find a new tactic and get under Rashad.

Since I didn't know if Kamden would be doing any pop-ups at my apartment, I told Rashad I would come over to his place. After taking a quick shower and oiling with cocoa butter, I put on a sexy sundress and white pumps. I made sure to spray between my legs with Pretty in Paris fragrance before I left and headed to Rashad's place.

Rashad stayed about twenty minutes away in Flushing and when I pulled up to his one bedroom condo, I sat in the car for a minute. Although Kamden had cheated, I still felt guilty for what I was about to do. For months my heart was only with Kamden. I wasn't thinking about anybody else. Now, after the way he had hurt me, I only wanted to feel good.

Pushing the thought of Kamden out of my mind, I turned off the engine. I tapped lightly on the door and after a few seconds, Rashad came to the door wearing jeans and a red button up polo shirt. This time his hair wasn't braided, but pulled back in a neat ponytail. He smiled when he opened the door.

"Hello beautiful, good to see you again," he said kissing me on the cheek.

"Good to see you too. Thanks for inviting me over."

"Thanks for coming."

Rashad's house was nice, although it was a typical bachelor's pad. It wasn't decorated or anything, just had cream furniture, a flat screen TV, and a video game system. He led me into the dining room to a small card table.

"I can order us some Chinese food if you're hungry. Want something to drink?"

"I'm not hungry, but I will take a drink." I said putting my purse on the table and taking off my jacket. "How have you been?"

"I been cool... kickin it, you know how it is."

"I do."

Rashad brought me a coffee cup and poured some wine in it.

"Sorry about the coffee cup. I know you're a wine glass woman, classy."

"It's not about the type of glass, it's about what's in it."

Rashad laughed as he poured himself some wine.

"My type of girl."

He pulled over a chair and sat down next to me.

"So tell me about yourself."

"What do you want to know?"

"Whatever you want to tell me."

I ran down the list of things about myself I thought Rashad should know: raised by my father, no mother, one sister, one nephew, went to school for pre-law, favorite color green. I really wasn't interested in talking, we could've done that over the phone. Rashad must have sensed my irritation.

"You don't seem like you're in a talking mood."

"You want me to be honest?"

"That's always better."

"I didn't think I was coming over here to talk."

A smile spread slowly across Rashad's face.

"Well damn, you get straight to the point don't you?"

"I think you will appreciate the fact that I'm a woman that knows what I want."

Rashad bit his lip.

"Well I think you will appreciate the fact that I'm a man that knows how to please a woman that knows what she wants."

Rashad held my hand as he led me up to his bedroom. We didn't even get through the door before he pushed me up against the wall and grabbed my neck. I dropped my purse and my heart started beating fast. I didn't know whether to run or fight, but when he put his lips on mine and gave me a deep, passionate kiss, I was turned on instead. He left one hand around my neck as the other began to roam my body. My knees got weak as he squeezed between my legs and made my kitty start to purr.

"Take me to the bed," I ordered in a light whisper.

"Nah… Wait a minute."

Rashad got on his knees and put his hands up my sundress. He pulled down my thongs as I pulled up my sundress without bothering to take off my pumps. Throwing one of my legs over his shoulder, he started kissing my lower set of lips as I threw the dress across the room. I moaned and rubbed his head as I heard him licking and slurping and whispering how good I tasted. I could barely stand on my other leg, so I put it on his other shoulder. Just when I was on the verge of cumming, he stopped and made me stand up again.

"Come here," he said grabbing my hand. I was confused as we walked past the bed and unlocked the door to his balcony and let in the cool evening breeze.

"What are you doing?"

"I always wanted to fuck somebody out here," he said with a sly smirk on his face. "What, you scared?"

I didn't answer, just sat down in the patio chair and opened my legs wide. He smiled as he pulled a condom out of his pocket.

"Damn, I like you more and more by the second."

Rashad took off his clothes and slid the rubber on as he walked towards me. My legs were shaking because he was big and I didn't know what to expect. He grabbed my neck again as he slid inside of me and I could tell this aggressive sexual behavior was a fetish of his. He looked me up and down as he went in and out of me, slowly at first, then picking up speed as I put my legs as high as I could in the air, ignoring the weight of my white pumps.

What he was doing to me was something like sweet torture. It hurt, but at the same time he was hitting a spot deep inside of me that made me cry out loud enough for neighbors to hear. He took his hand from my neck and covered my mouth gently so no one could hear my screams. I wasn't used to the rough sex that he seemed to be a fan of, but I could definitely see myself getting used to it. Putting my legs down and wrapping my arms around his neck, I pulled Rashad's head down and slid my tongue in his mouth. Just when he was getting into the kiss, I bit his lip with enough pressure that it wouldn't hurt, but he would definitely feel it. He gave me a low growl and looked me right into my eyes.

"Damn, I like that. Bite me again."

This time I bit his neck and he pushed deep inside of me yet again, and we both cried out in unison from pleasure. I was almost there and I pulled him into me making him pound in and out of me harder until he hit that deep spot again and I let out a loud shriek as my body shook before it went limp. He cried out, too, before he threw his head back and came into the condom. Putting his hand on the back of the chair, he took a few minutes to catch his breath before he grabbed my hand and we went into the room quickly. We were sure we had been heard, the last thing we wanted was to be seen, too. We both collapsed on his bed and fell into a deep slumber.

I awoke in the middle of the night to my phone ringing. Rashad was asleep beside me and didn't stir at all, but I got up, fished it out of my purse and answered quickly so it wouldn't wake him.

"So you blocked my number huh?" Kamden yelled into my ear. He had called from another phone number. "Where the fuck you at?"

"Stop calling me."

"I been riding by your apartment and you haven't been home all night."

"And stop riding by my fucking apartment. Get a life Kamden, and stop calling me. I mean it."

I ended the call and laid back down. It was four in the morning and although I didn't plan on staying all night at Rashad's house, I was tired and too comfortable to move. His warm, naked body felt good beside mine and I fought the urge to snuggle up to him. He had done my body right though, and I was going to make it a point to keep him on my recent call list often.

When I woke up the next morning, I was in Rashad's bed alone and his comforter was covering my naked body. I stretched, then got out of bed, grabbing his green t-shirt and putting it on. I was acting like I'd known this man for years as I left out of his bedroom in search. He was downstairs in the kitchen taking food out of a carry out bag which immediately made me smile because I was starving.

"Good morning sleepyhead," he said, smiling at me.

"Morning. I stole your shirt."

"It looks better on you anyway. I went and got us some

food. Since you didn't eat last night, you must be starving."

"I am," I answered, nodding my head.

I sat at the table and Rashad opened a styrofoam box with an all meat omelet and hash browns in it. My stomach was doing flips and I couldn't wait to eat, but I waited for him to get his food and get settled across from me.

"So, you figured out that I can't cook yet?"

I laughed.

"I hadn't paid attention."

"Yeah, I'm no cook. I can boil water, pop popcorn...oh, and I make a mean hotdog."

"Oh a hot dog? That definitely takes work."

"Don't sleep on my hot dogs, I'm telling you, they'll make you slap ya momma!"

I covered my mouth because it was full of food and I couldn't stop laughing.

"Just like a man, bragging about making hot dogs."

"You can cook for me, I won't complain."

"You put it down on me like you did last night and I just might do that."

"So you sayin' you gonna chill with me again?"

"That depends on if you want my company."

"Hell yeah I do. As a matter of fact, did Kapri talk to you about Miami?"

"Yeah, but I don't know if I'm going to be able to make that trip."

"Why not?" He asked, taking a drink of his orange juice.

"I just don't have the money like that right now."

"So, what if I make sure you get there...will you go then?"

"You would pay for me to fly to Miami for the weekend? You don't even know me like that."

"I know that I like a woman that knows what she wants, and I know the couple of times we have kicked it, it's been cool. I wanna go with someone I know I'll have fun with. So will you?"

"I'll think about it."

"If you come, I can guarantee you will enjoy the whole weekend. I'll make sure of that."

"I'll definitely think about it then. Now eat your food before it gets cold."

CHAPTER 13

When I got home later that day I took a long hot bath and got into my bed. I had to work the following day and I planned on spending the whole day in my bed eating junk food and watching Lifetime. I needed something to help me forget about my miserable life. Staying the night with Rashad had been so much fun, and he made me feel good, but it was back home and back to reality. Single. Brokenhearted. Cheated on. And no Kamden. My heart got heavy every time I thought about seeing Rebecca at his door.

I awoke at two in the afternoon to someone knocking. It took me a minute to get out of my bed and put on my robe. I peeked through the peephole expecting to see Kamden, but instead it was a tall, dark man with long dreads hanging down his back. I reluctantly unlocked the door and stood face to face with a dark brown muscular man two times my size. He stared down at me with his brown eyes and I immediately felt like a little girl.

"Hi Daddy. What are you doing here?" I asked, without

making eye contact with him. I hadn't seen him in a few months and him showing up at my door unexpected had me confused.

"I talked to Shauna and she said you were going through some things and I wanted to make sure you were okay."

I was looking at my Daddy like I didn't believe him, but I moved aside and let him in anyway. He looked around my house as if he was in search of someone, but there was no one there for him to find.

"So, what's going on Naomi?" He asked, sitting on the couch and crossing his arms. I couldn't read his facial expression.

"I just broke up with my boyfriend."

"It's pretty sad that I didn't even know you had a boyfriend, but go ahead and tell me what happened."

I rolled my eyes.

"If this is what you came over here for Daddy, you can turn around and walk back out. I am not in the mood for those smart ass comments."

"First of all watch your damn mouth little girl," Daddy barked. I immediately calmed down because despite everything, I was still his daughter and I knew he had no problem knocking the hell out of me.

"I'm not trying to be smart, I just don't understand how and why you would completely cut your father out of your life. I did everything I could for you and Shauna after Denise left us and you know that."

"Yes Daddy, I do know that."

"So why is it that we are where we are right now? You

really blame me for you mother leaving?"

"I think you know more than you let on."

"Denise was selfish, and I'm sorry you don't want to believe that. She wanted to live her life and not be tied down by a man and kids. That had nothing to do with me, you or your sister."

"I won't believe it. I remember the day she left. I remember waking up and being at the kitchen table and she said she was going to get me and Shauna milk and oatmeal. She kissed us both and said she loved us and would be right back-"

"And did she ever come back Naomi?"

I didn't want to cry because I didn't even know if I had enough tears left. This was why my father and I had stopped speaking. We had argued about it months ago, but I refused to believe my mother just up and left us for no reason at all.

"Did you ever look for her? Call the police and report her missing?"

"I didn't need to. She packed her things that night Naomi; they were already in her car. When she left that morning to go to the store she never had any intention of coming back."

I sat on the recliner with my head in my hands trying my hardest to hold back tears. My father came over and rubbed my back.

"Naomi…I swear to you if there was anything I could've done to keep your mother in your lives, I would've done it. I never wanted Denise to leave, I was still in love with her. I'm not going to tell you I was perfect, but I wanted my family. I'm so sorry that this hurt you so bad all these years."

My Daddy started stroking my hair and I started crying uncontrollably. Not only about my mother, but about Kamden and the way he had broken my heart. It seemed like all I ever did was cry, but it did felt good to be crying in the arms of my Daddy. Deep down I'd missed him.

"It's okay baby girl, I'm right here. You always have your Daddy, don't ever forget that. I don't care what we go through."

I nodded my head as my Daddy tried his best to calm me down. After making me take deep breaths and getting me a bottle of water, we sat down and talked about Kamden.

"I really thought he was the one Daddy. I loved him. And he played me not once, but twice."

Daddy nodded as I lay my head on his shoulder.

"He's young, and sometimes when men are young we do stupid things. We don't realize when we have a perfect woman in front of us and we tend to still do the things we want instead of focusing our attention on making the woman we love happy. That's typical, I'm not saying it's right, but it is very common. So you have two options: take him back or leave him be."

"I don't want to be hurt anymore. I thought he was going to change this time."

"Do you still think he will?"

I shook my head. I wished he would change and be the man I needed him to be, but the reality was he was a dog and he was never going to care about anybody but himself.

"Then maybe it's best you leave him be. I'm your father, so you already know I would prefer for you to do that, but I also know love is a complicated thing. You can't help who you fall in love with, and I don't think you would be this tore up about it if you weren't in love with him."

"I am."

"Then if you are going to be with him you need to make him work for you. Don't settle for any bullshit from him because what you allow will continue. If you take him back after what he's done and act like nothing happened, he'll cheat again because he knows you'll only take him back anyway. It's okay to be in love, but don't be a fool…especially for a man that isn't your husband and not planning to be."

I nodded my head again and smiled up at my Daddy. Sitting and talking to him made me realize how much I missed him and needed him in my life. I still had so many unanswered questions about my Mother, but they would be answered in time. Life was too short, and taking into account that either of us could be gone tomorrow, it wasn't worth it.

Daddy kissed me on my forehead and pulled me closer to him

"I missed you baby girl. It was killing me not to talk to you. I don't want us to do that again."

"Me either. And I'm sorry for all the things I said I never meant to be disrespectful-"

"You were angry. I know you didn't mean any of it. No matter what you're my daughter. That's why I came over to check on you after I talked to Shauna."

"What did she tell you?"

"That you were at her house drunk and crying your eyes out."

"She was exaggerating Daddy," I said with a smile.

"Yeah right she was," he said laughing. I closed my eyes and inhaled his scent... cherishing this moment like it would be my last even though I prayed the last time with him would never come. Before Kamden, or any other man I had loved my father, and there was still no other man on Earth that could take his place or that I would love more.

"You need anything from Daddy Naomi?"

I nodded my head as a small smile spread across my face.

"What?"

"Chocolate French toast."

Daddy laughed that deep laugh that came from his stomach like what I had said was the funniest thing he'd ever heard. For him, this moment had to be confirmation that I was and would always be his little girl. No matter how angry I got at him, he was the man whose arms I would always run back into because there I knew I would be safe. He continued to smile to himself as he got up and went into the kitchen to start making my favorite meal.

CHAPTER 14

"So, who is going to be tuned in with their family tomorrow for the annual parade?" Keith Sweat asked through the speakers of my small radio that sat on my counter in the kitchen. Although he was addressing millions of listeners all over the world, it seemed as if he was asking me personally. His deep, sexy voice filled my kitchen as I busied myself, preparing the macaroni and cheese, green beans, yams, and corn. I was making sure everything was ready to be cooked the next morning and fresh for Shauna's house and The Sweat Hotel was exactly what the doctor ordered to get the job done. My phone rang just as I had started cutting up my sweet potatoes. I didn't know the number on the screen, but I answered anyway.

"Hello?"

"MiMi," Kamden said softly. "Are you still coming to my family's house tomorrow for Thanksgiving?"

"What do you think?"

He took a deep breath and didn't say anything for a

minute.

"My Momma really wants to see you again. She's going to be disappointed when she finds out you're not coming. Aunt Ginger too. My Uncle Amos has been wanting to meet you."

"Well, why don't you take Rebecca? I'm sure she'll jump at the opportunity."

"I never took Rebecca to meet my parents because she was never as important to me as you. I want to marry you one day Naomi-"

"Oh Goodness, save this for someone who wants to hear it Kamden because I don't anymore. I don't want any more of your promises and I don't want to be a part of your dreams. We are finished."

"My family was looking forward to seeing you again."

"Well, I guess its time for you to tell them what a lying, cheating, two-timing, no good dog you are...then they'll understand why I won't be passing the potatoes at the table tomorrow."

"MiMi, is there anything I can do to get you back? I know I keep fucking up, but I want you."

"Kamden, tell your family I said have a happy Thanksgiving and you have a good life. Do not call me from your phone or anybody else's ever again, *we are done*. There is nothing you will ever be able to do to change that."

I ended the call and put my phone back on the counter. I was shocked Kamden had even wasted his time calling me. It was obvious he hadn't told his family what had happened between us, but it was time for him to come clean. Either way, I wanted nothing else to do with him.

"Hi little sister!" Shauna said when she opened the door.

"Hi Sissy!" I exclaimed handing her the two aluminum pans I was carrying and going back to my car to get the others. I returned and put everything on the kitchen counter where Shauna had already begun laying the feast out.

"Everything should be done in about ten minutes, and Auntie Sueann and Tarrissa should be here soon with the yeast rolls and desert."

"Cool, I'm starving. I didn't know Daddy was putting something on the grill."

"You know Daddy never misses the opportunity to spark up the grill," Shauna said putting the food I'd brought in the oven. "He told me ya'll made up."

Shauna had a huge smile on her face like it was the best news she had heard in a long time.

"Yeah we did. He came by to check on me after you told him I was over your house drunk and crying my eyes out," I shook my head. "You know you got a big mouth."

"Is that what he said happened?" Shauna asked with her mouth wide open. "I did tell him, only because he asked about you just like he always does when he calls me."

I shrugged my shoulders. It didn't matter how Daddy found out about me and Kamden. I was just glad we were on good terms again. As if on cue, my Daddy entered from the patio dressed in blue jeans and a green sweater and a Kiss the Cook apron. He was carrying a pan of ribs and smiled as soon as he saw me.

"Naomi, hey baby girl. Happy Thanksgiving!"

He came over and gave me a kiss and I slipped a rib off the pan.

"Just like when you were little," he said laughing and putting the meat in the oven. "Where the hell is Sueann? I'm ready to eat."

"She called Daddy, she's on her way," Shauna said.

Daddy sat down at the table and we sat and chatted until Aunt Sueann and Tarrissa arrived. Daddy, Shauna and I all met them at the door to help them carry in the food and drinks they had bought. Tarrissa handed me a black bag and gave me a wink. I looked inside and there were three bottles of wine and a fifth of tequila. I smiled like a child who had just been given a handful of candy and put our stash in the refrigerator. Shauna and I could always count on Tarrissa to bring the alcohol.

"Well it's about time you got here," Daddy said giving Aunt Sueann a kiss on her chubby brown cheek. She smiled, showing off that same large grin Daddy had.

"Oh hush Davis, you're the one who asked me to cook all this desert. Perfection takes time as Mommy always said," she replied, opening her long black jacket and revealing the brown turtle neck sweater and dark blue jeans she was wearing. Daddy took her coat and put it in the bedroom with the others. "Where is Jalil?"

"He's with his Daddy for Thanksgiving this year. He gets Christmas with me this year, then we switch next year," Shauna responded. "He picked him up earlier."

Aunt Sueann pouted a little, the washed her hands in the kitchen sink. We all joined hands and said grace before we made our plates and enjoyed our holiday meal. The food was delicious and I was enjoying being comfortable with my own family. Once I was finished with dinner, I got a plate of Aunt Sueann's desert complete with pound cake, banana pudding, peach cobbler and even a slice of apple pie. I felt like a pig, but it was one of the few times I could be greedy and get away with it. I made a secret promise to myself to go to the gym soon and work off all I had gained.

"Well Davis, you outdid yourself on that grill this year. Those ribs were almost falling off the bone!" Aunt Sueann said with a toothpick sticking out of her mouth. I could tell she was full.

"Aunt Sueann, you can't give up already. You haven't gotten any of your desert."

"Oh yes I have. Somebody had to be the taste tester."

We all laughed and continued talking and watching the football game on TV. My father had a smile on his face like he was truly happy at the moment. I was hoping my presence had something to do with it. Daddy had always taught us to thank God for all the things we were thankful for on this holiday. I knew without a doubt mending fences with my father was right at the top of that list.

CHAPTER 15

"Anything else you need me to do before I leave today?" I asked my boss, Attorney Judith Lynn Prospect. She was sitting behind her desk staring into one of her big law books with reading glasses on.

"Just hand me my briefcase and that notepad over there on that table and I am good," she said pushing her curly black hair behind her ear. I retrieved the items she'd asked for and put them on her desk.

"Thanks for everything Naomi, I'll see you tomorrow morning."

"I'll see you then!"

I kicked off my heels as soon as I made it home from work. My black business suit came right after and made a trail to the kitchen where I stood in my pink Victoria's Secret bra and panty set and poured me a much need glass of Riesling. Judith had ran me all day and I was mentally and emotionally drained. All I wanted to do was lie around in my underwear.

It had been a few weeks since Thanksgiving and I was feeling a lot better. Although I was still hurting over my heartbreak with Kamden, I was enjoying myself with Rashad and getting lots of money from Joe. Once again I was having fun and trying my best to forget about Kamden. He wasn't giving up though, so his name continued to be on my blocked list.

Laying out on my couch, I called Rashad who answered on the first ring.

"Hey sexy lady, what are you up to?"

"Nothing. Just got home from work, laying in my bra and panties."

"Ooh, that sounds sexy. I wanna see you like that."

"Maybe I'll send you a picture."

"A picture is good for now, but I want to see you in person. Don't you miss him?"

"Yes I miss him. You know he knows exactly how to make me happy."

"So come play with him. He misses you."

Rashad loved referring to his dick as if it was another person, and I had no problem entertaining that fetish. It turned me on in some ways because it was something I hadn't experienced before. Rashad was an expert at talking dirty, and I loved every minute of it.

"I just got off of work Rashad, and I'm tired."

Somebody started knocking on my door, and I jumped off the couch and looked through the peephole. I wasn't real surprised when I saw Kamden standing there, but I was shocked to see his mother standing beside him. It would be easy to tell Kamden to go to hell, but I couldn't just be rude to his mother like that. She had nothing to do with Kamden's actions.

"Rashad, I'll call you back," I whispered in the phone before I ended the call without waiting for his response. "Who is it?" I yelled through the door as if I hadn't already looked through the peephole.

"MiMi, you know it's me," he said sounding pitiful. "I got my Momma with me because she wanted to see you."

"I have no problem seeing *her* Kamden, but, you, *you* can go to hell."

He didn't say anything else. I went quickly to my bedroom to throw on some sweats and opened the door. Roxanne stood there beside her tall son, wearing leggings, a large black sweater and tall black boots. Her hair was in a bob with a swoop of bangs covering one eye. She gave me a warm smile before she wrapped her arms around me.

"I missed you at Thanksgiving MiMi."

"I missed you too Roxanne," I said sincerely. I was happy his mother seemed to like me so much.

Kamden tiptoed in behind his mother, and I glared up at him making it known I wasn't letting him in because I wanted to.

"You have a very nice place MiMi," Roxanne complimented, looking around my apartment.

"Thank you. Would you like something to drink Roxanne?"

"No thank you boo. How have you been doing?" she asked sitting next to me on the couch. Kamden sat in the recliner looking uncomfortable like a naughty kid at parent teacher conferences.

"I've been doing better. Mostly trying to stay busy and keep myself entertained."

"Well first, I definitely wanted to come over and see how you were doing. Kamden didn't want to bring me, but I made him. I hope you don't mind."

"No, I don't mind that you're here Roxanne, it's him that I have the problem with."

"Look, I know my showing up here, getting in the middle of ya'll business is weird and I am so sorry for that. But I, like you MiMi, have a good head on my shoulders. My son told me what happened and I know you think he is a no good, lying, cheating dog," she said looking at him with an evil glare. "And I don't blame you because he is…just like his father."

Roxanne took a long pause as she glared at her son with disgust all over her face.

"I know it's not easy being in love with someone who only cares about himself… I did it most of Kamden's life. His father wanted a baby, so I had his baby. Well, then he wanted to travel, so I left our baby with my sister to travel the world with him. And the whole damn time he had two other families. And the reason he wanted to travel the world so bad was to mess with the other women in between his baby mommas."

Roxanne laughed a little, perhaps at herself and how young and dumb she had been.

"I blame myself a lot for the way Kamden treats women. I was the first woman he trusted and I abandoned him for a man. Then, I let his father run in and out of my life for so many damn years thinking it was better to have some of him than nothing at all. So I can understand why he would have issues when it comes to relationships."

I listened politely, but I didn't know where Roxanne was going with her speech. I wasn't going to have mercy on Kamden because he showed up with his Mommy.

"I'm not here to tell you to forgive him or anything like that. I realize what he did was unforgivable. But I did want you to get a chance to tell him how you felt so he could know the pain he put you through. Hopefully it changes him and he won't continue his disgusting behavior. I know my son really loves you and sometimes losing that first love is what a boy needs to become a man."

I glared at Kamden who sat in my recliner with a stupid look on his pathetic face. Every time I looked at him I thought about him having sex with Rebecca and it made me sick to my stomach.

"There isn't really much I have to say to you Kamden. Deep down I knew you wouldn't change and that you would hurt me again, but I wanted to believe you loved me and that I would be enough for you."

I fought back tears and continued.

"I'm not. You need to go be with Rebecca, because she won... again. There is obviously something she has that I don't because she always gets you. And honestly, I don't want to fight for your love anymore because it's not worth it. The man I'm meant to be with won't make me fight for his love. He will fight for me and for the family we create."

Kamden didn't say anything, he just stared at me. I was almost surprised he wasn't talking to me, but maybe he was getting the hint that I really was through. Sitting there talking to him about it was hard, but I needed closure. Roxanne was right, Kamden did need to hear how he had hurt me, and I hoped it wasn't going in one ear and out the other like it had all the other times. Maybe someday Kamden would change, but it was sad I wasn't going to be the one he was doing it for.

"So guess who just left my house?" I said into my cell phone. Roxanne and Kamden had left and I couldn't wait to talk to somebody about their visit.

"Who?" Kapri asked. "Rashad?"

"Guess again."

"Don't tell me it was Kamden," she said with disgust all in her voice.

"Yes, but he wasn't by himself."

"If you tell me he showed up at your apartment with that bitch I am going to drive to his house and kick his ass myself."

I laughed at my ride or die friend.

"Hell no, he knows better than to bring her to my house. He brought his mother with him."

"His Mom? He really showed up at your door with his mother like it was his first day of kindergarten?"

"She asked him to bring her because she wanted to talk to me and give me a chance to say what I wanted to Kamden. Kind of make him face what he did."

"Okay, I guess I get it. How did it go?"

"It was fine. I didn't really have much to say to him," I said taking a bottle of water out of the refrigerator and taking a drink.

"Well obviously. Did he say anything to you?"

"Not really. I think he knows its over and there isn't much he can say. I mean, he was caught with his pants off literally with the girl in his house. Case closed."

"Good. And I think for your sake it should stay that way. Every time you get back with Kamden he hurts you. You're much better off without him."

I wasn't sure if that was what I wanted to hear at the moment, but I thanked Kapri anyway and changed the subject.

"So what are your plans for Miami? Is Brock all excited?"

"Yeah he is. He plans to fuck me on every beach we walk across."

"Well, that's romantic. Sounds like my type of vacation."

"Well it could be your type of vacation if you came with Rashad. I'm sure he wouldn't mind fucking you on the beach."

"I'm sure he wouldn't, but I can't go to Miami with him."

"Why not? You said he was really nice and you liked him."

"He is, and I do… but it doesn't feel right."

"Why wouldn't it feel right? You and Kamden *are* done right?"

"Yeah, I told you we are."

"So there's nothing to worry about. You and Rashad are so cute together, and me and you would have so much damn fun in Miami! Walking up and down the street in our swimsuits, getting drunk and partying all night, fucking on the beach... girl, please tell me you're down. I don't want to go with anybody else but you."

Kapri was selling the vacation and it was sounding better and better. However something about going to Miami alongside Rashad wasn't making me jump up and down. I liked him, but I wasn't sure if it was enough to take vacations and see the world with.

"I'll think some more about it Kapri, but I honestly don't think I'm going to make this one. But we will plan a trip soon, just you and me and we'll party and get drunk all day and night."

"Alright," Kapri said sadly. I could tell she wasn't completely satisfied with my answer, but she knew she would have to accept it. I ended the call with her, poured myself a glass of wine and went to take a bubble bath. Roxanne and Kamden's visit really had me thinking about my future. Eventually I wanted to be somebody's wife and I wasn't going about it the right way entertaining all these men. Being valued was much more important than being desired and ultimately that was what I wanted. If I was going to be some man's wife one day I had to start being a better woman, not for me, but for the man that would someday be my husband.

CHAPTER 16

After Kamden and Roxanne's visit, I couldn't get Kamden off of my mind. Things between us had been damn near perfect until the night Rebecca answered his door. There had never been another man I loved more than Kamden and getting over him was harder now that I had seen him. Love in my opinion is a drug addiction. No matter how much it hurts, it is still needed and wanted… and Kamden was my drug.

In an attempt to get my mind off of Kamden, I decided to call Joe. I knew he would not only enjoy my company, but also pay well so I could buy myself something to make me feel better.

"Naomi, hi beautiful. What did I do to deserve this call?"

"Oh, stop it. You know I miss you, you haven't been calling me lately," I pouted as if he could see me.

"I been a little busy baby, but you've been on my mind. I thought you were tired of the old man."

"Never tired of you Joe. You're so sweet and take such good care of me, how could I ever be tired of you?"

He laughed, and I knew I had him right where I wanted him.

"Joe," I purred. "What are you doing? When are you coming to see me?"

"You want me to come see you?"

"Yes. I just told you I missed you," I said getting annoyed. "It's fine, I understand if you can't come over-"

"No, I aint never say that baby, slow ya roll. Let me make a few calls and I'll be right over to see you."

A sly smile spread across my face.

"You hurry up and make those calls baby, I'll get some food ready for you."

I ended the call with Joe and freshened up to prepare for his visit. Joe always made sure he took care of me, so I liked feeding him and making him happy. He was at my door within the hour with my favorite: Reese's cups. I knew it was because I was vulnerable, but I had missed Joe and was genuinely happy to see him standing at my door. He looked good for his fifty three years, especially with his hair and beard cleanly shaved. I let him in and locked the door behind him. He immediately planted a kiss on my lips.

"You are absolutely stunning," he said staring at me. I blushed and laughed the compliment off.

"Sit down and take off your shoes, and I'll get your food."

I left Joe in my living room and went to get the plate of leftovers I had warmed up out of the refrigerator. He grinned when I sat the massive plate of meatloaf, green beans, mashed potatoes and cornbread in front of him along with a tall glass of lemonade. I sat beside him and watched him devour the plate as if he hadn't eaten in days.

"You sure can cook baby. Who taught you how to cook like this?"

"My Daddy. He's a great cook."

"Your Dad can cook," he said as if he was thinking about it. "Not a lot of men can cook."

"That's very stereotypical of you."

Joe shrugged his shoulders.

"It's true. What, your Mom didn't like to cook?"

"No... she did... She just didn't cook for us," I said quietly.

Joe continued his meal not noticing the change in my demeanor at the mention of my Mother. I erased the thought of her the way I always did and focused on Joe. I rubbed his back and shoulders as he ate, treating him as if he was the only man in my world. When he finished his food, I took the plate into the kitchen, returned and straddled him.

"Tell me how you been baby, what's going on in your life?"

"Same. Working like a dog, that's about it."

"How much that lady pay you to work for her."

"She pays me good enough money for what I do. Why?"

Joe rubbed my back, stopping to squeeze my butt.

"Because a woman like you shouldn't be working. You should be home looking pretty and cooking those meals."

"Yeah, wouldn't that be nice?" I laughed.

"I'm serious. I would take care of you. Pay your bills, take you shopping, travel and let you see the world. That's the kind of life I could give to you."

"Oh yeah?" I asked kissing Joe on the neck. "And what about your wife? Huh? Are we going to send her postcards from Venice Beach? Meet her at Somerset Shopping Center and all hold hands and walk through the Gucci store? Yeah, that's really gonna go over well."

"I mean, if my wife was gone, like out of the picture?"

"Are you saying you're going to divorce her?" I asked in disbelief.

"I've been thinking about it. It's something about you Naomi... I haven't felt this way in a very long time. She doesn't make me feel this way anymore."

"Joe... I think you need to think about this, that *is* your wife."

"I know, but sometimes you fall out of love... and you fall in love with somebody else."

Joe kissed me and slipped his tongue in my mouth. I closed my eyes and let him wrap his arms around me, holding me close to his large warm body. I couldn't lie, my mind was in a million different places and I was enjoying the way he was making me feel, so I had completely forgotten about our conversation, and that he had just professed his love to me. My temperature started to rise and I knew it was time to give Joe what he came over for.

Standing up, I took off my clothes to give him a strip tease. I watched as his pants started to rise showing how he was responding to my body. I straddled him again, this time fully nude, and slowly unbuttoned his shirt.

"You wanna go in my bedroom?" I asked softly, sliding the shirt off his shoulders. He nodded his head and followed me into the bedroom where he also undressed and climbed on top of me. Sex with Joe was much different. He was older, so he wasn't as energetic and creative as Kamden, or as rough as Rashad. He tried his best to please me, and sometimes he came close, but I knew it was because I wasn't exactly physically attracted to him. Old men were just something I wasn't into. The only reason I kept him around was to serve his purpose: boost my self-esteem and give me money. However when we got to my room, I threw him on my bed and gave him the sexiest look I could muster. I climbed on top of him again and helped him take off all of his clothes. After I slid on a condom, I put him inside of me and began to ride him so I could move the process along as quickly as possible.

Joe immediately started moaning and grabbing my breasts and I wasn't on top of him three minutes before he made a noise that made me know he was finished. He pulled me next to him and gave me a kiss on the lips.

"You're so good baby, I swear you're the best."

I smiled and nodded my head.

"I know Joe, I know."

CHAPTER 17

I stepped into my black pumps Monday morning and business as usual, grabbed my black briefcase and checked over my black and white pantsuit. As I swung open the door, my demeanor immediately changed. Kamden was sitting on one of the lawn chairs that sat on my porch wearing black sweat pants and a red hoodie, the hood pulled low over his head and his hands deep inside his pockets. I rolled my eyes.

"How long have you been here?" I asked, turning my back on him to double lock my door. The plan hadn't changed just because he had come by with his mother, I was still going to ignore his worthless ass.

"About an hour or so. Can we talk, please?"

"I'm late for work, so you can talk in about the time it takes for me to walk to my car."

"MiMi, you do not have to be to work for another thirty five minutes," he said getting up and following me as I headed towards my car.

"Okay, I just don't wanna talk to you," I said over my

shoulder. Kamden grabbed my arm forcing me to turn around.

"MiMi-"

"My name is Naomi, Kamden. Stop *fucking* calling me MiMi."

"Okay, can we talk?"

"Why? What do you have to say? Do you really think there is anything you *can* say about what happened on your birthday?"

"No," he said softly. "I know I fucked everything up... again... and it's probably nothing I can do to make it better."

I was nodding my head before he even finished the sentence. When I looked at him, all I saw was him coming out of the bathroom that night and it literally made me sick to my stomach.

"I was wrong, I know that. But I will do anything, anything at all to make it up to you."

I turned and continued to walk to my car. It was the same old bullshit! How could he even come to my doorstep with that after what he had done?

"Baby, I know you think I'm saying the same old shit, but I mean it, I swear I do."

"So what was last time for you? A game?" I asked reaching my car and opening the door to put my purse and briefcase inside.

"No it wasn't a game. I made a mistake, people make mistakes MiMi. I know I hurt you and I know it was wrong, but I love you, not her. She doesn't mean anything to me, she's jealous of you because she knows I will never have the feelings for her that I have for you."

Hearing him say Rebecca was jealous of me was a little satisfying, but at the same time it didn't mean as much as I thought it would. Kamden was acting like it was a privilege to be with him, but I was so much more than the girl on his arm.

"MiMi can you say something to me please?" He begged, holding my car door so I couldn't close it. By now I was sitting inside my car and so done with his apologies. He knew that holding the door was the only thing that was keeping me from driving away.

"There is nothing for me to say. I'm tired of this Kamden. I'm tired of you feeding me fairy tales and dreams a bunch of bullshit that will never come true. You are who you are and you're not going to change, and I'm not going to give any more of my life waiting for you."

Kamden bit his lip a little, but it didn't turn me on the way it used to. He looked like he wanted to cry, but he didn't. He just stood there staring.

"Can you close my door now?" I snapped, and when he did, I took off and left him standing in the parking lot. It would be so much easier to get over him if he would just stay away, but he was making it very clear he wasn't going anywhere.

I had spent most of the morning nibbling on fruit so by lunch I wasn't even hungry. I was only half surprised when I saw Kamden walk through the office door. He had changed out of the lounge clothes he'd had on earlier and was now wearing jeans and a black button up coat. When he saw me he gave me a half smile, but I didn't return it.

"I see you got my gift," he said nodding his head at the large edible arrangement he'd sent that sat, partially eaten on my desk.

"I did. You know you didn't need to send me anything because it changes nothing between us," I said crossing my arms.

"I know, I understand you're mad at me still and I don't blame you. I just want to talk. I know it's lunch time, can I take you out to get something to eat?"

"I'm not hungry."

"Then I'll get you some ice cream. Please baby, I just wanna talk to you for a minute."

"About?"

"MiMi, you know what I wanna talk to you about."

I stared at him for a very long time before I reluctantly grabbed my purse and told Judith I was leaving for lunch. Kamden held the door as I followed him out to his truck. He didn't start it. We just sat there as he stared at me, probably trying to figure out a way he could apologize to me that wouldn't be like all the other times.

"Just tell me what you want me to do. I'll do anything if I can just have you back."

I thought about it for a long time before I replied.

"I don't really know how to answer that Kamden. Honestly, I feel like a fool. You have made a fool of me so many times and I'm so tired. I can't trust you anymore so how can I possibly continue on a relationship?"

Kamden just nodded his head with that same pitiful look on his face. He knew what I was saying was the truth. No woman deserved to be cheated on; men just didn't understand how much that hurt.

"I want to be married one day. I want a life with someone who I can trust that is going to be faithful. I don't want to have to be worried every time you walk out the door, that's not the life I want. There are plenty of women in this world who don't mind being with a man that cheats. You can go find one of them because that will never be me."

He didn't hesistate.

"I don't want you to be like that. I want to be faithful to you and I want to be your husband. There is no other woman I want to be with and I am so sorry for all the times I hurt you. I know you can't see yourself trusting me. I'm asking you to try to give us a chance, to give me another chance. I promise I won't hurt you again, I hear everything you're saying and I understand. What happened with Rebecca was not planned, I hadn't been talking to her and it didn't mean anything to me at all. I don't love her, I swear I don't. I love you."

I was listening to what he was saying and I could tell he was sincere. I didn't want to be a fool again, but I loved him so much it was so hard to walk away. Nobody knew me or could handle me like Kamden and being in a relationship with someone other than him scared me. Not only that, it could also mean going through the same thing with someone different who didn't love me like Kamden.

"You were in a relationship with her for a year-"

"And I left her for you! I told her I was in love with you and I didn't want to be with her anymore. I ignored her calls, text messages and everything. I hadn't even talked to her until she showed up at the door on my birthday and I was drunk. That's the only reason anything happened."

"Right, blame it on the alcohol, T-Pain," I said sarcastically.

"I'm not, I did what I did and I'm sorry. I'm not blaming anybody or anything for that. I just want you to know I fucked up, I realize that and I won't do it again."

"Kamden-"

"So you tellin' me you don't love me no more?" He asked already knowing the answer.

"I do love you Kamden but-"

"You really about to be done with me? Over some bitch that I don't even care about?"

I didn't know what to say, so I just shook my head. Kamden was emotional and that made it even harder for me to reject him. Even after all he'd put me through I was still so in love with him and I really didn't see myself ever loving anybody more than I loved him.

"I don't know Kamden."

"Baby, don't walk away from everything we had. You know I can change, and I want to for you. All I want is one more chance to have you back. I will make you the happiest woman in the world every single day of your life."

I wanted to believe him with everything inside of me. He looked like he was telling the truth, but I could only hope he was. His eyes told me he was sincere, but I thought he was every time.

"I need time to think about it Kamden. You hurt me badly-more than once."

"The way you looked at me and the way I made you feel on my birthday hurt. I haven't even been able to sleep. I don't ever want to see you like that or make you feel like that. But if you need time to think I can give you that."

I nodded my head and opened my door, but Kamden grabbed my arm.

"Wait... Let's go get that ice cream I promised you."

When Kamden dropped me back off at the office, I was feeling a little better about him than I had before. When we went to get the ice cream we didn't discuss our relationship at all, just talked and laughed like we were teenagers. Kamden always had the ability to make me forget his wrongdoings and although his latest discretion had been one that was hard to handle, I could feel myself thinking about him more. As I finished my work day, it was extremely hard to keep him off of my mind and I was kicking myself for it too. I couldn't understand why I just couldn't walk away from him, or how I had fallen so deeply in love in the first place. It was like he had some kind of power over me because no matter how mad I got at him, all he had to do was pull on my strings a little and he would be right back in my good graces.

I threw my keys on the living room table along with the rest of my edible arrangement before I plopped on the couch. Already comfortable, I didn't want to move, so I just kicked off my heels and turned on my TV. Mentally I was drained and I needed to relax and watch a little TV to try and get rid of my stress. I unbuttoned my blouse and laid back in my bra and skirt as I watched afternoon talk shows. Almost an hour went by before my phone rang.

"Hey Daddy," I answered.

"Hey baby girl, how was work?"

"Work was work, you know how it is. How are you?"

"I'm doing good. I just wanted to call and check on you, make sure you didn't need anything."

"Making your rounds," I said laughing. "No I don't need anything, thank you Daddy. Have you talked to Shauna?"

"Not yet, but I'm calling her as soon as I get off the phone with you. So what's going on?"

"Nothing. Work was busy, that's all."

"You sure? You sound different, not as happy as usual."

"It's Kamden. He's been trying to apologize all day. He sent me an edible arrangement today and came to take me to lunch…"

"Damn. He's laying it on thick for you baby," Daddy said laughing.

"I know! But it's like now I can't get him off my mind."

"Well, as your father, you know I want to tell you to look the other way and not date anybody else ever again."

We laughed.

"But I know when it comes to love, things don't always turn out the way you want them to. You have to make the decision that will make you happy. Just remember, it's hard to be in a relationship with someone you don't trust no matter how much you love him. A relationship without trust is like a cellphone without service... you can only play games."

"Wow. I like that Daddy," I said nodding my head and thinking about what he had said.

"Thanks. I read it somewhere, I think it was Facebook."

"Daddy, you do not have a Facebook," I said in disbelief.

"Yeah, I got one a couple of months ago. Got about three hundred friends already," he stated proudly.

"Daddy... do not go around telling people that, especially people who knows you are my Daddy."

"What you mean? Half of them make up the three hundred people on my friends list!"

"Oh my goodness, bye Daddy!"

We both laughed for what felt like forever.

"I love you baby girl, enjoy the rest of your day."

"Enjoy yours too, Daddy."

CHAPTER 18

"I see you don't care about your sister anymore," Shauna said into the phone. I was sitting in the break room on my lunch break praying over the tuna fish sandwich and fruit I had packed to eat.

"That is not true."

"I can't tell. Why haven't I heard from you? What have you been up to?"

"Not a damn thing."

"Well you must be up to something to be MIA like you have been. If I didn't know any better, I'd think you got back with Kamden."

I didn't say anything, because I was trying to find the right way to tell her that was exactly what I had done. I knew she wouldn't be happy.

"Naomi, don't tell me he worked his way back in."

"Shauna-"

"No, Naomi, please don't be a fool. Do you remember

what it felt like that night he cheated? The way you said that bitch smiled at you when she answered the door? He didn't just cheat on you, he *humiliated* you."

"Yeah Shauna, I remember okay. I know what he did and so does he. I love Kamden so much-"

"So much that you're willing to let him make a fool of you. Well, don't come crying at my door again when he does."

"Don't worry Shauna, I won't."

Fuming, I ended my call with her. She had a lot of fucking nerve talking shit about me after everything her baby daddy had put her through before they finally broke up for good. I just felt like the pot was calling the kettle black and it pissed me off so badly my head was spinning. Taking my frustration out on my sandwich and fruit, I threw it into the trash and went outside to take a quick walk before I went back to work.

My relationship with Kamden was far from where it was supposed to be. He knew he had a long way to go before I could trust him again. We had been talking on the phone and texting a lot, but we hadn't actually seen each other since he showed up at my job and took me to get ice cream. I hadn't invited him back to my apartment, and I refused to go visit him. Today, however, we were supposed to meet at Blackstone's for a date. I showed up early wearing a skinny jeans, black pumps, and a black and white blouse. My hair was pulled up into a bun and I wore gold hoop earrings. Kamden showed up wearing jeans and a white and navy blue button up shirt. I stood to kiss him.

"Hi baby. You look gorgeous," he said wrapping his arms around me holding me longer than just a few seconds.

"Thank you."

We sat together in the booth and looked over the menu. He wrapped his arm around me and kissed me on the cheek.

"You're so beautiful," he said gazing at me as if we'd just met for the first time.

"Thank you," I said, unable to stop blushing.

"I have so much I wanna say to you, I don't even know where to begin."

"I know where you should begin."

"MiMi, I know I was wrong. My birthday I got drunk with my friends and she showed up. That doesn't make it right at all, I know the history with Rebecca makes everything so much worse."

"I just don't know what she has that I don't," I admitted. "It's like every time we're happy and working on building something she comes slithering back in and takes you away from me."

Kamden shook his head.

"I had a moment of weakness. That doesn't mean she took me away from you. Nobody can ever do that. You have my heart MiMi, and nobody can ever take that away, I promise you that."

After we placed our orders, we resumed our conversation.

"Kam, I'm not gonna lie it's going to be a lot of work to get our relationship back where it was. I already feel like a fool for taking you back again."

"I know, but I'm going to make it worth it. I'm going to

prove to you that I can change and that I can make you happy. I'm never going to cheat on you again or hurt you. I wanna marry you and have a family with you. I've never felt that way about any other girl."

Everything Kamden was saying to me, I had heard before. He had a way with words and knew just what to say to melt my heart. I could only hope that what he was saying was the truth and that he really was ready to change. The last thing I wanted was to be made a fool of and prove Shauna right.

Kamden and I ate our food and continued to talk about our relationship. I still wasn't absolutely certain that I was making the right decision with taking Kamden back, but I loved him so much that I wanted it to work. All I could do was pray that Kamden was telling the truth this time.

"So what about this one?" Kapri asked, coming out of the dressing room wearing a navy blue bikini. It showed off her toned and tanned body and I gave it a thumbs up.

"Okay, so it's between this one, the black and red one, and the red, white and blue one," Kapri said twirling around in the mirror to look at herself from every angle. She had her hair pulled back in a ponytail and her nails and feet were freshly painted for her trip to Miami. She was bummed I wasn't going, but she dragged me out to help her look for bathing suits.

"I think you should get that one, and the black and red one. They look the best on you."

"I think so too."

Kapri went back into the dressing room and emerged

again wearing her jeans and purple t-shirt. She carried the bathing suits in her hand and after she put the other one in the return pile, we went to the register. She paid for her items and we walked out of the store and back into the mall. It was a Friday evening, so it was full of people hustling about starting their Christmas shopping or buying their outfits for the weekend. We made our way to the food court where we got Chinese food before we slid into a booth.

"What time does your plane leave?" I asked, taking a sip of my soda.

"Five thirty in the morning, which means we have to be at the airport at like three thirty," Kapri replied shaking her head. "I'm going to sleep the whole flight."

"Yeah, waking up that early. You probably won't even go to sleep you'll be so excited."

"I'd be more excited if you were going with me. I know Rashad was bummed you weren't going. He kept telling me to try and get you to change your mind."

"Well, I almost did."

"I wish you would've. I don't even know this chick Rashad is bringing. She better be cool. I don't want my vacation ruined. I've been waiting for this for so long."

"Everything will be fine," I assured her. I wasn't surprised Rashad was taking someone else to Miami because we had talked about it. I was glad he was still going and had a date. It showed me he hadn't gotten too attached to me, which was good, because I also needed to focus on my relationship with Kamden.

"How are things with you and your Dad?" She asked,

browsing through the racks as she headed to the register.

"Things are much better. He calls at least every other day to check on me and talk. I'm happy. I missed him."

"I know you did. And you know you can't blame him for what your mother did. The questions you want him to answer are questions only *she* can answer."

I nodded my head because she was right. I wanted so badly to blame somebody for what my mother had done, and since she wasn't around, it was easy to take all of my anger out on my Daddy, which was unfair.

We threw our trash away and went downstairs and out of the food court. Kapri wanted to go to a shoe store to buy sandals and heels before we left Genesee Valley. She picked out some shoes and continued to chatter about how excited she was to be lying on the beach with a Tequila Sunrise. Deep down I was jealous, and the more she talked about it, the more I wished I was going with her to Miami. It was then that I realized I had made the choice to not go because of Kamden and our relationship and it made me resent him more. After all he had done, I was still willing to give up a fun vacation even though he had already proved himself to be untrustworthy time and time again, but being on a trip to Miami with anyone other than Kamden wouldn't feel right. Even though I was missing out on sunshine, pretty beaches and fruity drinks, I had made my decision to stay home and work on my relationship with Kamden so unfortunately that was what I had to do.

CHAPTER 19

The days went by; they became shorter and colder. Snow began to fall leaving soft, white mountains on the ground. If the weather didn't signal Christmas was near, the constant replaying of Donny Hathaway's, *This Christmas,* definitely did. I was trying to get in the holiday spirit by decorating my three foot Christmas tree. It was less than a week away and I was feeling like a scrooge. Hopefully putting up the tree would make me feel better, but if not, buying gifts for my nephew definitely would. I was in love with his innocence, and I missed the days when my only worry was not getting what I wanted for Christmas.

My phone rang and Shauna's name popped up on my screen. We hadn't been talking as much since I got back with Kamden because she wasn't as supportive as I needed her to be. Although I didn't blame her, I was still her sister and I wanted her to be there for me like I was always there for her.

"Hey Shauna," I answered.

"Hey Sissy, what are you doing?"

"Putting up my little Christmas tree and trying to cheer myself up. I'm in a funk and I don't really know why," I said, hanging a small gold ball on the tree.

"Well I wanted us to talk. I feel like we've been distant and I don't like it."

"Me either. I miss you."

"Miss you too."

There was a pause as I waited for her to say something else. Since she was the one who called me, I figured she had things she wanted to get off of her chest.

"I can stop by your house. I'm on my way to pick up Jalil. I have a few minutes before I have to be there," she finally said.

"Okay, I'll unlock my door for you."

Shauna was walking into my apartment in less than five minutes as if my house was her intended destination anyway. We both smiled at each other and I stopped fussing with the Christmas tree and sat next to her on the loveseat.

"Shauna, I feel like things have changed between me and you because I decided to give Kamden another chance. I know you were mad and I understand, but at the end of the day, I'm your sister and you should still be there for me no matter what."

"Yeah, I was mad you got back with him. It's not like we have anybody else, it's just you and me. And you know when Momma left I looked after you and I'm overprotective. I let Kamden get away with a whole lot when it comes to you and I'm done giving him chances."

Shauna took a deep breath and I was beginning to think this talk was going nowhere.

"But, you're right," she continued. "You are my sister and I should still be there for you. And you know no matter what I say, I will be. When I get mad I talk all that 'don't call me when he hurts you' crap, but you know I'll be the first one ready to whoop his ass if he does."

I nodded my head and laughed because I knew she was telling the truth. Shauna and I hardly ever got into arguments, and Kamden was a stupid reason to even start. Shauna had to understand that I was going to make my own decisions regardless of how she felt, and I had to understand that she loved me and would always voice her opinion whether I wanted to hear it or not.

"Love you Shauna," I said wrapping my arms around her like I did when we were little. She hugged me back and I was relieved that in three minutes we resolved an issue that had stopped us speaking for weeks.

"Have you started shopping for Jalil yet?" I asked, trying to lighten the mood.

"Started? Girl, I'm damn near done! Have you seen the store's right before Christmas? I beat the rush this year!"

Shauna did a little dance and I bust out laughing at her.

"Well you have to tell me what you got for him so I don't go out and get the same thing."

"You can come over and wrap gifts, that way you know exactly what I bought."

"I can help you wrap gifts, but I'm not doing all your dirty work for you."

"I don't expect you to. Cool, I'll let you know when I get the wrapping paper and you can bring a bottle of wine."

"Wine?"

"I never wrap gifts without it," Shauna said getting up and stretching. She had to go pick up Jalil from his father at a certain time and go home and get him ready for bed.

"You going to Kamden's house for Christmas?"

"Yeah, since I missed Thanksgiving. They have brunch on Christmas Eve, so I'll be by your house Christmas Day."

"Okay, well I love you. Call me later," she said giving me a kiss on the cheek. She left me alone again in my apartment with a half-decorated Christmas tree and a little bit of holiday spirit.

Waking up next to Kamden on Christmas Eve was nice. It was kind of cold, so we were cuddled up close to each other and I could feel his hardness pressing against my backside. I grinded against it a little bit, just to tease him, and sat up. Things between us were tense, but I was really trying to see if it was going to work. I couldn't lie, I didn't feel as strongly as I did about him the way I did before, or as confident about our relationship, but I did love him. For that reason, I wanted to make things work with him. I wasn't ready to give up on the dream I had of marrying him and starting a family.

I went into the bathroom and turned on the shower. Kamden came in to use the bathroom and as I took off my silk nightgown, he watched me. I stepped into the shower, letting the hot water hit my body. I didn't plan to take long because I wanted to be on time, but once I got in, the water felt so good I never wanted to get out. Kamden got in behind me and rubbed his fingers up and down my body.

"You think we got time to get in a quickie before we go?" He asked holding his dick in his hands.

"No, we do not have time! That's why we woke up so late. If you wouldn't have woken me up out of my sleep, we might've gotten some rest."

"Don't act mad now. All I heard last night was 'harder Kamden, give it to me harder'," he said trying his best to imitate me during sex. I couldn't stop laughing as I washed my body and got out so it could stop distracting him. I still had to do my makeup and hair. I didn't have time to play with his ass.

When he finally got out, I was in the mirror with the towel wrapped around me and my makeup case sitting on the sink. He slid by me, making sure to touch me when he did, and went into my bedroom to get dressed. I finished my makeup and threw some curls in my hair before I started getting dressed too. By the time I finished, Kamden was sitting on the couch flipping through channels on the TV and waiting for me to get ready. He smiled when I entered the room.

"Damn, you look sexy baby," he said as if I had on a lingerie set instead of the black and brown sweater dress, leggings and boots I was wearing.

"Thank you," I said putting on my other my other gold hoop earring. "You ready?"

Kamden turned off the TV, grabbed his wallet and keys as I got my purse off of the couch where I had left it, and followed him out the door.

When we arrived at his Grandmother's large brick home I was in awe at how beautiful it was. It was three stories and sat right off a huge lake. It was frozen now, but I imagined it was even more beautiful in the summer. This was the kind of house I imagined living in and raising a family and as soon as I walked in, I was overcome with a warm, loving feeling like the family that resided there was nothing but. We were greeted by a short, gray haired man with a large beard. He was smiling at us and made his way over and hugged Kamden.

"Uncle Larry! What's going on man?"

"Aww, nothing nephew! Getting better looking every day. This must be MiMi, I heard she was a pretty little thing," he said holding his hand out and looking me up and down.

"Yeah Unc, this is my girlfriend, so you stay away from her. I know how you are. I'll have my eye on you."

"Yeah you better youngsta, because this one here sho is one good looking lady! You got good taste nephew, real good taste."

I laughed and blushed at the same time, thanking old Uncle Larry for his compliment. He winked at me and smiled again before Kamden grabbed my hand and pulled me away to meet everybody.

"My Uncle Larry was a player back in his day. He always trying to steal somebody woman," Kamden said laughing. He introduced me to his cousins and a few of his uncles who were all gathered in the living room watching football. The closer we got to the kitchen, the more women we started running into. His mother was sitting at the table cutting potatoes and talking to an older woman. She got up and hugged me as soon as she saw me.

"MiMi! I'm so happy to see you," she beamed. She was hugging me tight too, and I was glad that she was so excited to see me.

"It's good to see you. How have you been?"

"Well, you know me. I'm always gonna find a way to be good. The question is, how are you and my son?" She asked looking from me to Kamden.

"We've been better. I'm trying to give him a final chance."

She nodded her head and smiled at me.

"He better make it right. I already told him I didn't want anybody else but you to be my daughter in law."

After hugging me again, she also gave her son a hug and a kiss on the cheek. She sat and continued to cut the potatoes as Kamden introduced me to the other woman at the table.

"MiMi, this is my Aunt Gertrude, my grandmother's sister."

The woman stood up and she towered over me by a couple feet. She was extremely tall and I looked up in awe at the older woman who clearly had to be a supermodel in her younger days.

"Aunt Gertrude, this is my girlfriend MiMi," Kamden said finishing the introduction as Aunt Gertrude looked down at me with a stern look on her face.

"MiMi, nice to meet you dear," she said shaking my hand as if she didn't really want to touch me. "I've heard quite a bit about you. Nice to finally put a face to the name."

"Nice to meet you too. You are beautiful."

"Why thank you sweetie! Oh, you're a doll," she said patting me on my head as if I was a dog. I could tell already this was the aunt that thought she was better than everybody. If her mannerisms didn't reveal that, her apparel definitely did. She was wearing a cashmere sweater and diamond studs. She clearly had not come to help cook. I forced a smile and let Kamden lead me into the spacious kitchen where Aunt Ginger was standing over the stove stirring a pot and a woman in a pink sweat suit and apron sat at the island cutting fruit. Her gray hair was pulled into a bun in the middle of her head and she was wearing pearl earrings.

"Hi Big Momma," Kamden said leading me over to where she was sitting and kissing her on the cheek. "This is my girlfriend MiMi, the one I was telling you about."

"MiMi, I'm so glad you decided to come, she said getting up from the stool and giving me a hug and kiss on the cheek. "I know my grandson is something else, but it's not all his fault. His Momma acted like a damn fool half his life and his Daddy was no better."

"You'll have to excuse my mother MiMi, whatever she's thinking comes out of her mouth," Ginger interjected.

"I've been on this earth eighty one years- I earned the right to say what the hell I want."

She stopped and gave me a warm smile.

"But I don't wanna scare you away, so just pay me no attention when I say something crazy."

"Trust me, it'll take a whole lot more than some honesty

to scare me away. I have thick skin."

"Kamden, she'll fit right in. You like to cook baby?" Big Mama asked putting her hand on my shoulder.

"Yes ma'am."

"Leave her in here with me Kamden, we need to talk about you while you're not standing over us listening. Go on and watch those sports with your cousins."

Kamden gave me a kiss on the cheek and did as he was told. I got the eggs and milk out of the refrigerator like Big Mama instructed me and started the French toast. Pulling up a chair and sitting at the island with her, I began to crack eggs in a large bowl.

"Roxy told me why you didn't show up for Thanksgiving," Big Momma said picking up her small knife and continuing to cut the melon in bite sized pieces. "I don't blame you. I told that boy he was an idiot for pulling something like that. He is too damn old to be running around playing games like a teenager."

The more Big Momma talked, the more I liked her. She was raw and honest and definitely somebody I could see myself talking to when I needed advice. I wished I had a grandmother like her, but both of mine had died when I was young.

"Kamden is my grandson and I love him more than my next breath, but if he can't get his act together and do what he is supposed to, you go and find somebody who will. You are too young and beautiful to wait around for some boy to be a man."

Big Mama shook her head and cut the melon with a

frustrated look on her face. She was taking Kamden's actions against me very personally and I didn't quite understand why until she started talking again.

"Bernard cheated on me a long time while we were married."

Aunt Ginger abandoned the stove and looked at Big Momma like she too was shocked at what she said.

"Back in my day things were different. Bernard went to work and paid all the bills. It was my job to keep the house clean, cook, and make sure the kids were taken care of. I didn't know how to live on my own and get a job and pay the bills because he did all of that."

By now, neither myself nor Aunt Ginger was cooking anything because we were hanging on to Big Momma's every word.

"So when I found out about his affair, I didn't confront him, I didn't stress him out. He was a good provider for me and my children so rather than leave and make a hard life for myself and my kids, I let it go on and lived a good life off of his money. See, people like to act like marriages used to last so long because we honored the vows so much we didn't leave once we found out our husbands were having affairs, but in reality it was all about survival. Don't get me wrong, those vows are sacred, and anytime you make a promise to God, it should be upheld. But I don't think God intended for a woman to stay home and endure the pain of knowing her husband is out with other women."

Big Momma had finished cutting the fruit and was staring absently out of the window as if she was reminiscing instead of having a conversation with me and her daughter.

"Men back in the day would have a whole other woman and family across town and the women would shop at the same grocery stores, go to the same banks and the children wouldn't find out until their father was dead and gone. Why do you think I was so adamant about you not dating Florence Everett's boy Ginger?"

Ginger's mouth dropped open and I couldn't believe I was sitting in on such an intimate conversation between mother and daughter. Big Momma blinked a few times to come back to reality and smiled at me.

"So, I said all that to say, nowadays a woman's happiness and financial support no longer has to come from a man. You are all you need and if Kamden is not the one, eventually you will find the one who is."

I nodded my head and started beating the eggs. I had no idea what to say after a story like that and I knew this was one of those times I needed to just listen and not speak.

"Momma," Ginger said, wiping her hands on her apron with her mouth still hanging open. "You never told me that before."

"No need to shame the dead," Big Momma said, putting her hands on her hips. "But there are some things women need to know."

CHAPTER 20

Kapri had been busy with school and work so we hadn't had any time to hang out since she had gotten back from Miami. She must have been feeling overdue for some best friend time because she popped up at my house a couple of days after Christmas with a small gift wrapped in red and gold wrapping paper and a little gold bow.

"What is that? I know it's not for me," I said putting my hands on my hips as she kicked off her shoes, and walked past me into my apartment.

"It's your Christmas gift silly," she said putting her purse on the table and unzipping her purple and black coat. She sat on my couch, still wearing her black hat and scarf over her jeans and black sweater.

"No, I'm not taking that. I didn't get you anything Kapri," I confessed locking my door.

"The last time I checked that's not what The Season of Giving is all about. Now come open it before I slap you."

I rolled my eyes and playfully snatched the small box from

her hands. After ripping the wrapping paper and opening the small box, I was staring at a pair of 14 karat gold hooped earrings.

"And you better not lose those. I'll be checking," she said smiling.

"Thank you, Kapri! I feel so bad because I did not get you anything," I said with a pout as I gave her a big hug to thank her for the gift.

"I don't care about that. Your friendship is my gift all year long. Now go put them in your jewelry box, you know I hate to get mushy."

I went to put the earrings up, and plopped back on the couch next to her.

"So, I wanna hear all about Miami. How was it?"

"Miami was so much damn fun! We stayed right on the beach and you could just walk up and down the street all day. You literally wore your bikini everywhere you went. I should've bought all of them that day at the store!"

"Seriously?"

"Yes girl. I'm glad my body is popping," she said laughing.

"And how are things between you and Brock?"

Kapri scrunched up her face in a way that made me think what she was about to say wasn't going to be good.

"We're still seeing each other, but you know how it is."

"No... how is it?"

"There's always butterflies and sparks at the beginning then things start to wear off. It's starting to wear off between Brock and I."

"Why?"

"Guys always change. At first they're all about the flowers and the candy and asking how you feel and what you need…then when it starts getting serious, it all slows down until it eventually stopped altogether."

"Did you talk to him about it?"

Kapri shook her head.

"If I have to talk to him about it, it's already a lost cause."

"Why do you always do that Kapri?"

"Do what?" She asked, getting up and going to the kitchen, proving that she obviously could not handle the heat. I got up and followed her because she already knew she was not getting off that easy.

"You always give up on a relationship before you even give it a chance."

"I do not."

"Brock, Jeff, Jamal… and that one guy that used to deliver your mail, what was his name?"

"His name was Vince and what you are saying is not true," she said taking a can of pop out of my refrigerator and grabbing my family sized bag of barbeque chips from out of the pantry.

"Yes it is. And do you know what I am starting to think?"

"No, you better not say it!"

"I'm really starting to think-"

"Shut up Naomi."

"-that you are-"

"I don't wanna hear it," she sang, trying to cut me off again.

"-afraid of commitment."

Kapri turned and looked at me with a heinous look on her face.

"I knew that's what you were about to say! I am not afraid of commitment, I'm afraid of no good ass men."

I let out an unwilling chuckle because Kapri had such a way with words. I couldn't believe the things that came out of her mouth sometimes.

"Okay, I understand. But is there really something no good about a man getting comfortable in a relationship and forgetting to keep the romance on? That's why you nip that shit in the bud now before it gets to where it's gone forever."

Kapri crunched on her chips and rolled her eyes before she answered.

"I don't have time for that shit Naomi. A man is supposed to be just that, I shouldn't have to tell him what he is supposed to do... keep me happy."

"Do you think you're perfect Kapri? I'm sure you don't do everything you're supposed to do all the time."

"Maybe I don't, but I notice. I don't wait around for somebody to tell me."

I could feel the conversation getting a little intense, so I changed the subject.

"Did you go see your parents for Christmas?"

"I stopped by, they were leaving town like always, so I didn't get to stay long."

Kapri was one of the few people I knew whose parents were married. Although they'd raised her, they spent the majority of her life leaving her with her Grandmother because they were always on a plane going out of town, away from her. She held a lot of resentment in her heart for that, but still tried to go visit them.

"That's good though, at least you went by there."

"Next year, I'm not. Fuck them too, right along with these men."

I didn't dare make a comment and I was seeing my subject change obviously hadn't worked. Instead of trying to find a new topic, I put myself in the hot seat instead.

"I went to Kamden's grandmother's house for Christmas brunch."

"How was that?"

"It was cool. I loved his grandmother. She was so real and down to earth about everything. I wish I had a grandmother like her in my life."

"So things are good between ya'll again?"

"So far they are. I don't trust him and I'm still taking baby steps, but he's been good lately."

Kapri nodded her head and didn't say anything. Like Shauna, I know she wasn't happy I had decided to give Kamden another chance, but she would always be supportive no matter what.

"So you're not talking to the old guy anymore?"

"I still talk to him from time to time. I'm trying to let him down easy."

"You don't know what Kamden is going to do, so you need to keep him in your back pocket. He gives you good money when you see him."

"It's not always about the money."

"What, do you love him?"

"Hell no, but I think he may love me and that's the problem. I don't want to play with anybody's heart. He has a wife and children and seriously asked me if I would be with him if he divorced his wife. That's too much. Even if things don't work out between me and Kamden, it's time to cut him loose."

"Yeah, if he's talking about leaving his wife you gotta let that go. He'll really be thinking he has a chance with you and be mad when he finds out what's real."

"And he won't be able to go home because wifey gonna have the locks changed."

Kapri and I both fell out laughing and I was glad the mood was getting lighter.

"So, finish telling me about Miami," I said, sitting at the table with Kapri and getting a handful of chips. "How were the men? I know you were still looking."

Despite what I'd told Kapri, I didn't stop talking to Joe. He knew that I was with my boyfriend again, but he still used anything he could to come see me. One day, he texted me and told me he wanted to give me some money to go shopping. I already knew he was using that as bait to come and see me, and since I wasn't one to turn down free money, I quickly obliged. When he came over he had my Reese's cups and six crispy one hundred dollar bills and I was damn near drooling. Joe definitely had the romance on full shine so when he came in, he took off my panties, and put me on the counter. I didn't say anything-just gripped the candy and money as he buried his face into my coochie.

"You always taste so good and sweet," he said, as he lapped my pussy like a thirsty dog. I moaned and grabbed at my nipples as I grinded on his face. I'd made it clear we weren't about to have sex and he was cool with that, but for him, just making me cum got him off and what woman was going to turn down good oral?

CHAPTER 21

I tried to find my phone under my sea of covers and pillows in the dark. I had obviously fallen asleep with it in my hand and now it was ringing nonstop. Whoever was calling was hanging up and calling right back like something was wrong. When I finally found the ringing cellphone, it stopped. I had time to see four missed calls from Kamden, but before I had a chance to hit the redial button, he was calling me again.

"Hello," I answered as quickly as I could.

"Baby, I need to see you," Kamden cried into the phone. This was one of the very few times since I met him that I had ever heard him cry.

"What's wrong Kamden," I asked, turning the lamp on my nightstand on.

"Man, shit's crazy."

I waited for him to tell me what was going on, but all I could hear was him taking a bunch of deep breaths like he was trying to pull himself together.

"My Aunt Ginger is dead," he said sounding like he was in shock. My mouth almost hit the floor! I was just sitting and talking with Ginger a few days ago and now he was telling me she was dead.

"Aunt Ginger? Kamden, are you serious?"

"Baby, I need to see you."

"Yeah, I can come over there if you want me to," I said, already getting up and throwing on some clothes.

"Please? I was going to go be with my Uncle, but I just can't stand to look him in his eyes. I know he's going through hell right now."

"Yeah, you going to see him right now is probably not a good idea. Try to calm down-I'll be at your place in a minute," I said grabbing my purse and keys, slipping into my Ugg boots and walking out the door wearing my nightgown, and sweatpants underneath my green winter coat.

When I got to Kamden's house, he explained to me that his Uncle Amos had tried to wake Ginger up out of her sleep in the middle of the night and she wouldn't budge. They were thinking it could have been a heart attack, but there was no way to be sure. The only thing that was certain was Ginger, the sweet woman I had gotten to know who was more like Kamden's mother than his own, was dead and gone and he was a mess. We stayed in his bed all that day because he couldn't stop crying. I had never seen him like this. I didn't know what to say or do, so I just lay there and let him hold me and talk to me whenever he wanted to.

Later that day we got up and got ready to go to Ginger's house to be with the family. I still didn't think Kamden was ready to face it all, but he loved his Uncle Amos and wanted to make sure he was okay. Roxanne and Big Momma were both worried about him because they knew how he felt about his Auntie. So Kamden pulled himself together, got dressed, and led the way outside to his truck.

The mood was somber in the car as we drove to Ginger's house. I felt an incredible amount of sorrow. In the short time I had known her, Ginger was always sweet and loving to me and I just couldn't believe I was never going to see her again. Kamden was having a really hard time and when I pulled up to her house and parked the car, Kamden had tears streaming down his face. I took off my seatbelt and gently rubbed his shoulder.

"You okay baby, you need a minute?"

He wiped his face with his sleeve and shook his head.

"I'm alright," he said taking a deep breath. "I gotta go in there and see my Uncle. I know he's looking for me."

"Well I'm here for you, you know that. Whatever you need, just let me know."

"Thanks baby," he said forcing a smile. "I'm so glad I got you back."

I gave him a kiss and we got out of the car. He knocked lightly on the door and a middle-aged woman opened it.

"Kam, hey cuz!" she said, wrapping her arms around him. "How are you?"

"I'm tryna be strong. You know Aunt Ginger was like a mother to me."

"I know," she said rubbing his back. "She loved you so much."

We went into the house and there were people everywhere.

I had never been to Ginger's house before, but I felt right at home as soon as I walked into the door.

"Francine, this is my girlfriend MiMi."

"Hi MiMi. I've heard a lot about you. I live in Delaware so I haven't had the pleasure of meeting you, but my Mom had nothing but nice things to say."

"Ginger is your mother?"

Francine gave me a small smile making her light brown eyes squint. She nodded her head, her black curls bouncing at the top of her head. She was tall, like a model, which was the first thing I thought when she opened the door.

"I'm so sorry for your loss. She was such a beautiful woman."

"Thank you. I appreciate you saying that. We definitely need to sit down and chat later. Kamden is more like a brother to me so I need to get to know the girl who finally got his heart."

I could tell Francine was trying her best to be strong, but I could see the sadness in her eyes. My mother walking out on me was completely different than what Francine was going through, but I didn't know whether my mother was alive or dead. She didn't know it, but we had more in common than she thought.

"Daddy been asking about you all day. I think he's worried, so you need to go talk to him."

Kamden kissed Francine on the cheek and grabbed my hand. I waked with him around the house as he greeted his family. Everyone was expressing deep sorrow for him and it was clear he was extremely close with Ginger. We circled the house once, but never ran into Amos. I could tell Kamden was starting to get worried because he was squeezing my hand tighter and tighter. When we went into the kitchen there were people everywhere and I was starting to get nervous. I didn't like to be around so many people I didn't know, but Kamden was upset and needed to know that I was not going to leave his side.

"There he is," Kamden said dragging me through the kitchen. I knew it was because I was with Kamden, but it seemed like everybody was looking at me, not Kam. I held my head down and tried not to make eye contact with anyone until we were halfway across the kitchen.

"Kam!! I been looking for you-"

He started the sentence, but when I looked up, he stopped. We were staring into each other's eyes, but I don't think neither of us believed we were looking at each other. I started to feel lightheaded and now, it was me squeezing Kamden's hand. Amos was standing in front of *Kamden*, but the man that was standing in front of *me* wasn't Amos...it was Joe.

CHAPTER 22

Kamden wrapped his arms around Amos, but he just stared at me over Kamden's shoulders. I didn't know what to say or do, so I stood there shaking my head. I was in total shock that Joe and Amos were one in the same. If the wrong thing was said, so much could blow up in my face right in front of Kamden.

"I been worried about you Unc, how you doin'?" Kamden said, looking his Uncle in the eyes.

"Awww, son… I'm still in shock. I just can't believe she's gone."

"I know. You and Aunt Ginger were exactly what I wanted to have in a marriage. You were in love right until the end. You treated her like a queen."

I could tell Joe was uncomfortable about all of this being said in front of me because it contradicted everything he had ever told me. Joe was not in a relationship he was struggling to get out of and was obviously still very much in love with his wife. He struggled to find his next sentence.

"You know Ginger was special to me. I… I never thought about what my life would be like without her."

I couldn't stop my mouth from dropping open, but I quickly closed it before anyone noticed.

"I always thought Aunt Ginger would be here… When I get married, to meet my children-"

"I know son," Joe said, putting his hand on Kamden's shoulder.

"Oh yeah, Uncle Amos, this is my girlfriend MiMi," Kamden said pulling me closer to him. I forced a smile.

"Nice to meet you Amos."

"MiMi?" Joe said, giving me a strange look.

"Yeah, MiMi. I met Ginger a couple of times and she was always really sweet to me. I'm so sorry for your loss," I choked.

"Thank you MiMi. Ginger did tell me so much about you."

I could tell by the look on his face that he finally figured out MiMi was a nickname for Naomi this entire time. I was starting to feel sick.

"Amos, is this your nephew, little Kamden?" An older woman asked coming over to us.

"Yeah, Nancy, but as you can see, he isn't so little anymore."

"I see that," she said making her way closer to him with her cane. "And he sure did grow up to be a handsome young man."

"Thank you," Kamden said, giving her a charming smile.

"Excuse me Kamden, I need to go to the bathroom," I

whispered, giving Nancy a kind smile to let her know I wasn't being rude.

"It's upstairs down the hall, make a left, then a right. You want me to show you?"

"I can take her up there and show her son. Catch up with your Aunt."

"No, I'll be fine, the directions were clear. Thank you though."

I made my way upstairs as quickly as I could afraid that the contents of my stomach would come up all over Joe and Ginger's beige carpet. I followed the directions Kamden had given me and once I found the bathroom, I locked myself inside. I barely made it to the toilet before I started throwing up. I tried to be as quiet as I could because there were people everywhere in the house and since they didn't know me, it would be awkward if someone overheard.

After taking a couple of minutes to pull myself together, I rinsed my mouth out, washed my hands, and checked my appearance in the mirror before I opened the door. Joe was standing there leaning on the wall like he was waiting for me.

"Joe, what the fuck!?" I said as quietly as I could, partly because of the entire situation and partly because he had startled the hell out of me.

"What are you doing here with my nephew?" He whispered.

"Are you kidding me? You're seriously asking me that right now?"

"Yes! You didn't tell me you were dating my nephew."

"Well I'm sorry *Amos*," I said sarcastically. "I didn't know

Kamden was your nephew, not that that's any of your business."

"Naomi... I can't believe this. *You're* MiMi? You're his girlfriend!"

"Why are you worried about *this* now? You're wife just died, *your wife*! You're supposed to be grieving."

Joe didn't say anything for a minute and I started walking away, but he grabbed my arm.

"I did all of this for you... for us," he growled at me through gritted teeth.

"What the hell are you talking about?"

"I asked you before... many times, if my wife was out of the picture, could we be together."

I put my hand over my mouth and tears immediately started streaming down my face. I was hoping he wasn't telling me what I thought he was telling me. I could not be the reason that a woman as amazing as Ginger was dead, and I couldn't be the reason for Kamden's pain. She was like his mother.

"Joe, what did you do to her?"

"That's not important, the fact is she's out of the picture. Now you need to let Kamden know it's over," he threatened.

This was a side of Joe I had never seen before. He was sweating and talking with so much aggression that I was starting to get scared. I tried to walk away again, but he grabbed my arm more roughly this time and forcefully pulled me into what appeared to be the master bedroom...the room he had shared with Ginger. I felt extremely uncomfortable being in there and goosebumps covered my body like

Ginger's presence was near, listening to all of this unfold.

"Don't walk away from me, Naomi! Did you hear what I said?"

"Shhhh!! Joe, stop yelling. Someone is going to hear you."

"This thing you have with my nephew, how far is it going?"

"This *thing*? We're together. I'm his girlfriend."

"And so, you're in love with him?"

"I've been in love with Kamden for years now. Yes Joe, I'm in love with him and I'm not going to leave him."

Joe started shaking his head frantically like he was losing his mind.

"My wife is gone because of this, because I wanted to be with you."

"You are a maniac Joe! I'm out of here," I said approaching the door. As soon as I swung it open, I ran into Kamden who had a confused look on his face like he had been looking for me.

"MiMi? What are you doing in there?" He asked looking from me to his uncle with a suspicious look on his face.

"Toilet in the main bathroom was acting funny so I let her use ours. Decided to use this time to take a moment away from everybody," Joe lied quickly with a pathetic look of sadness on his face. I couldn't understand how Kamden didn't see through it. Instead he mustered up the bravest smile he could give his uncle.

"I know you're going through it Unc. Anything you need man, you know I'm gonna be right here."

"I appreciate that Kam," Joe said trying his absolute best

to look grief stricken. Kamden was eating right out the palm of his hand and I could feel myself getting sick again.

"Kamden, I'm gonna get ready to go home, I'm not feeling too well anymore."

"Well, you drove my truck here babe. I can drop you off, I need some air real quick anyway," he replied.

"Nice to meet you Amos, sorry again about your wife, she was a beautiful woman," I said not even looking at him. I turned and left the room, walking as fast as I could out of the house and to the car. I had to run because this had to be a bad dream… what had just happened to me was too crazy to be real.

I was perplexed the whole ride back to Kamden's house. His uncle has just implied to me that he had killed his aunt and it was all my fault: the woman he was in love with. Confessing to Kamden that I had been having an affair with his uncle was impossible. How could I tell him I was the reason for Ginger's death?

I didn't say anything the whole ride and followed Kamden quietly into his house. He put his keys on his small dining room table and started going through the mail pile. I kicked off my shoes and sat with my legs crossed on his couch, still in shock about what had just happened. He came and sat next to me, breaking the glare I had on his hardwood floors.

"You okay?" He asked, wrapping his arm around me and pulling me closer to him. I laid my head on his chest.

"Yeah. I should be asking you that."

"I'm definitely not fine, but I'm gonna make it. My

Auntie wouldn't want me to give up."

"I'm not going to let you give up," I said holding his hands.

"I love you," he said, kissing my forehead. "Aunt Ginger really liked you. She was so happy when she found out we were back together."

"I liked her too. She was always so nice to me... and she could cook some tacos!"

Kamden smiled for the first time in a long time.

"I'm gonna miss them tacos. Nobody could cook like her."

I lay on Kamden's chest and listened to him reminisce about Ginger and all the memories they had shared. I cried silently because I knew he would never forgive me if he found out the real reason for her death. I wanted to get up and run to my apartment and hide from the world, but Kamden was hurting and as his girlfriend, I needed to be there for him. Besides, I didn't have anything to worry about. Amos was the one who had killed Ginger, I really had nothing to do with it.

CHAPTER 23

The days leading up to Ginger's funeral were terrifying and uncomfortable for me. After finding out what Amos had done, I wanted to stay as far away from him as I could, but Kamden was making that impossible. He was having a hard time, so he wanted me with him through it all... including the choosing of Ginger's casket and the family viewing. It was the night before and I couldn't sleep a wink. Kamden had been sleeping like a feather lately, but it seemed he was finally getting some that night and I didn't want to wake him up with my tossing and turning. Sliding out of bed, I left the room quietly and went into the bathroom. I stared at myself in the mirror for a long time trying to make sense of what was happening to me. Just knowing what my actions had caused were making things unbearable and I knew I had to get it off of my chest. Not telling anyone what was going on was going to drive me crazy, but I couldn't bring myself to open my mouth and do it, so I decided to do the next best thing.

Grabbing a notebook and pen out of my junk drawer I

was convinced everybody had, I sat at my dining room table and started writing a letter telling exactly what had happened between Amos and I and how he had confessed to killing Ginger for me. When I started writing I had no idea who I would send the letter to, but I knew it had to be somebody that would believe me, understand, and not be judgmental.

"What you up doing, baby?" Kamden asked, coming into the kitchen and almost stopping my heart. Luckily he was going into the refrigerator and had not paid any attention to me writing in my notebook which gave me time to discreetly close it.

"I couldn't sleep at all, and I didn't wanna wake you up."

"I wasn't sleep, just resting," he said giving me a small smile and sitting across from me with a botte of water in his hands.

"Yeah, you haven't been sleeping much at all. You okay?"

Kamden shrugged his shoulders as he took a sip of his water.

"I feel… nervous. Like, I can't believe I'm about to look at my Aunt Ginger in a casket. It doesn't seem real."

I could hear the pain in Kamden's voice and although I was concerned and wanted to be there for him, I couldn't help but think about my letter that was within his arms reach and revealed everything I had done with his uncle. That was making me too uncomfortable to focus.

"You gotta get some sleep baby. I know it's hard for you, and you and your Aunt was close, but she would have wanted you to be strong, you know that. How's your mother?"

"She's making it. Putting on a good face for me, but I

think she's taking it real hard."

"See, you gotta be strong for your Momma. You know she's depending on you."

Kamden nodded his head and then chugged the rest of the bottle of water. He sat there for a moment before he stood up, stretched, then gave me a kiss the lips.

"Come to bed baby, I need you to put me to sleep."

"I'm on my way," I said, kissing him again. He left the kitchen, and as soon as I knew he was in the bedroom, I quickly finished up the letter, and addressed it to the person I wanted to send it to. Feeling a little better, I put the letter at the very bottom of my purse so I could drop it in the mailbox on the way to the funeral home, and went to bed to comfort my grieving boyfriend.

I stood in the back of the chapel as Kamden's family gathered around Ginger's casket, making sure she was dressed and made up to their standards for the viewing. They all admired her, and Roxanne ran out with tears in her eyes as Francine followed her. Kamden motioned for me to come closer and take a look and when I did, he grabbed my hand.

"She looks so beautiful. They did a really good job," he said.

I nodded my head in agreement and we proceeded to the back of the chapel to sit down. We were seated, and Kamden was telling me a story about when Ginger had spanked him for spying on Francine while she was on a date. Then an older couple approached us, and Kamden stood to greet them as I watched Amos standing in front of the casket with his head bowed. Seeing him standing over her crying as if he was a grieving widower was too much to bear. And it seemed nobody but me was noticing Amos' strange behavior or the way he was looking at me and Kamden with disgust 0on his face.

"Thank you for coming," Kamden said shaking an older gentleman's hand and kissing his wife on the cheek. She was wearing a silver and black pantsuit with silver accessories. There were dressed as if they were at the funeral instead of the viewing.

"Ginger was an angel in the church," the gentleman said with a smile. "Anytime we needed anything she was right there, no questions asked.

"She loved you too, Pastor Baldwin. She was always talking about your sermons and telling everyone how much they would gain by visiting your church."

"The church is definitely going to miss her, the Usher board especially. Nobody could whip those ushers in shape like Sister Ginger. That's why she was the president for three years running. It won't be the same without her."

Kamden hugged them both again and came back to where I sat in the chapel and slid next to me.

"That was Pastor Baldwin and his wife. Aunt Ginger was a member there for over 32 years."

I nodded my head and forced a smile. Sitting in the chapel, looking at Ginger in her black and red dress suit and a big red church hat pinned on the hood of the casket had me feeling so guilty. I knew she was only dead because of me and I would give anything to change that. Kamden rubbed my back trying his best to be strong for the many people who had come to pay their last respects to Ginger Peters.

Kamden had started talking to me about Ginger and as soon as he wrapped his arm around me, Amos let out a loud wail. Kamden jumped up to be by his side as I watched Amos' production from the back of the chapel refusing to move a muscle to show him any support. It was fake and I didn't know how much longer I could pretend I didn't know the truth. Ginger had always been so sweet and loving to me. After what Amos had put her through, he didn't deserve to live a happy life. I couldn't stand by and let him get away with it.

"Baby, you okay?" I asked, when Kamden came and sat next to me. He had tears in his eyes and looked like he was going to pass out. I made him take some deep breaths, then, when he looked a little better, I led him out to get some water. Seeing what Ginger's death was doing to Kamden was making me more crazy, and I knew I had to tell someone the truth before I lost my mind. What if the letter wasn't enough?

"This is just really starting to hit me MiMi," he said, as he shook his head and tried to wipe the tears before they fell. I pulled him close to me and hugged him, rubbing his back in an attempt to comfort him. Everything inside of me wanted to tell him the truth, but I knew we would never survive that. So I just stood there being the supportive girlfriend I was supposed to be while his Uncle sat in the chapel putting on a show and getting away with murder.

The hardest part about Ginger's death was the funeral.

Kamden insisted I walk in with the family so I was able to see them grieving up close and personal. Kamden was right, his mother was taking it the hardest. She was dressed in a black and white dress suit and black heels. It was the most dressed up I had seen her since I met her. She cried uncontrollably the whole funeral that she had to be carried out. It was then I had to cry too, not only because Ginger was such a good person, but because of the effect it was having on everyone she loved. I could tell their family would never be the same.

CHAPTER 24

It had been a long day at the office and all I wanted to do was pour myself a glass of Merlot and sit in a hot bubble bath. Attorney Prospect had given me some time off to be there for Kamden, but it was back to business and I'd spent the day cleaning up the mess the inexperienced temp had left while I was off. I was trying my best to get the thought of Ginger out of my head, but the guilt was taking over.

Cursing myself for not having a pair of comfortable shoes in my car, I walked slowly to my apartment trying not to put too much pressure on my aching feet. When I put my key in my door and walked in, I nearly jumped out of my skin when I saw Joe sitting in my recliner looking as if he hadn't shaved or showered in days.

"Joe, what the fuck are you doing here? How did you get into my apartment?" I asked, stopping in my tracks waiting for a reply that would never come. He stared at me for a long time, but still didn't say anything.

"JOE!" I yelled, making sure to keep one foot outside just

in case he tried something. If he would kill his wife, then he would have no problem killing me.

"I met Ginger when she was fifteen," Joe said as if that was the answer to my question. "And I loved her every day until the day she died...the day I killed her."

He said that last part really quiet like it was something he didn't want to say. I wanted to scream, but so far he wasn't doing anything wrong. He seemed like he had something to say, so I waited for him to continue.

"You made me feel a way I hadn't felt in a long time. You were young, sexy, freaky...all the things it seemed Ginger had grown out of over the years. Maybe I thought it was love, and maybe I was seeing things that wasn't there. But the bottom line is... I killed my wife so we could be together, and you're going to continue a relationship with my nephew?"

"Joe, I never told you to *kill* your wife. When you said out of the picture, I thought you meant a divorce or separation. I never thought you would kill her! And I had no idea Ginger was your wife! You lied to me about everything!"

"Well I did dammit, *I killed her,* now answer my question. Are you going to continue to have a relationship with my nephew?"

"Yes! I told you I love Kamden. You always knew I loved my boyfriend."

"Well see, that's where we're gonna have a problem," Joe said pulling a pistol out of his jacket and pointing it at me. "See because, I didn't kill my wife for nothing. Now shut the damn door!"

I did as he said quickly, and stood before him with the gun

still pointed at me. I was shaking all over and I was about to pee my pants. As soon as I saw the gun, I knew this was the end. There was no way in hell he was letting me leave that apartment alive. Not with everything I knew now.

"Sit down," he said, motioning for me to sit on my couch. I did, and sat with my hands in my lap praying the whole time that he wouldn't shoot me.

Joe stood up quickly and walked over to me.

"Give me your cell phone," he demanded. I fished it out of my purse and handed it to him, knowing I had just given away my lifeline and last hope for being saved.

"With my wife, it took a while for me to be able to go through with it. I mean, I loved her, but in the end she was in the way of not only you and I, but a lot of things that I planned to do before the end of my life."

He paused for a minute.

"Divorcing her did nothing for me. I needed her to die because I needed to cash out on the two hundred thousand dollar life insurance policy I took out on her so you and I could start our new life."

"Joe...please...you don't have to do this-"

"I was going to let you choose where you wanted to move. In the states, out the country, wherever you wanted. You weren't going to work, just sit at home and be my spoiled trophy wife."

"Joe, I'm sorry. But you misunderstood what I said-"

"I didn't misunderstand a damn thing Naomi, don't insult my intelligence like that.

My phone started to ring and we looked at it as if we both

wanted to answer it. He looked at the Caller ID, smirked a little, and refocused his attention back on me. The deranged look he'd had in his eyes a few minutes ago was replaced with the one of sorrow he'd had when I first walked through the door. That's when I knew I had to get out of there because he was obviously mentally unstable.

"I can't live with myself knowing what I did. She cried, and begged and asked why, and I didn't stop. Now I'm alone and I can't continue my days after what I did. And if you think for one second I'm about to just let you go on and be happy while I'm miserable after what I did for *you*, you're out your damn mind."

Joe came over to me and sat next to me, running the gun up and down my body like I'd always see in the movies. I never in my wildest dreams thought it would be happening to me in real life.

"I gave you a lot of my time and money and now you wanna act like I repulse you? Like you can't stand to sit and talk to me?"

"I didn't say that, but what do you think you're going to accomplish? If you kill me, you go to prison, and then you can't spend that life insurance money you killed Ginger for."

"Nobody is going to find out I killed you. If you disappear, who would even look my way as a suspect? Who would think to blame the poor widower who just buried his wife?"

I shook my head.

"You are not going to get away with this-"

"It doesn't really matter. If anybody ever does find out I

killed Ginger, it'll be too late anyway."

I didn't know what Joe meant by too late, but I was terrified. I had never seen a gun in my life, and now I had one pointing right at me, then rubbing my body in sexual ways. I didn't like the feeling of not being in control, especially with my own life on the line.

"You can't just lie to people and play with their hearts and think there won't be consequences."

"I never lied to you about anything. You knew I had a boyfriend that wasn't going anywhere, so what would make you think that you and I would ever have anything more than what it was?"

Joe continued to shake his head frantically and I knew it was because I was right. I may have been a little more flirty than I should have been, but I would not take responsibility for Ginger's murder.

"You killed Ginger because you *wanted* to! You trying to blame me is not going to take away what you did."

"I want you to stop talking," he growled. He sat next to me and pointed the gun directly at me and again, I thought I was going to lose control of my bladder.

He looked disoriented, like he didn't know what his next move was going to be. My phone rang again and I almost jumped up to answer it, but Joe had a look on his face that told me I better not move a muscle or it would be the end of my too-short life. I sat and watched my phone until it stopped ringing wondering who it was that had tried to reach me. I was silently praying somebody would stop by to visit or check on me, but nobody ever came. Joe rambled on and on about Ginger and how I had deceived him.

"The saddest part is that you don't care," he said, twirling the gun in his hand as if it was a toy. "I treated you good and you don't even care."

I could tell the more he talked about it, the angrier he was getting. Maybe he was finally realizing that he couldn't bully me into loving him even with a gun pointed at me. I didn't know what he was going to do next, but I did know if he really wanted me dead, I would've been gone the second I walked in my door.

"My wife is gone," he said throwing his hands up in the air. "And my life is forever changed because you made me feel things that I thought were real."

I let him talk and didn't open my mouth because I didn't know why he didn't understand what I was saying.

All of a sudden he started crying uncontrollably. I looked frantically for something to defend myself with, but I knew attacking him would only make things worse. He stared at me with tear stained eyes and the look on his face was blank; he wasn't even comprehending what was going on. My heart started beating fast because I could tell *he* didn't even know what his next move was going to be.

"That woman gave birth to my children, took care of me while I was sick, was by my side through everything… and I killed her!"

He was sobbing now and a part of me wanted to feel sorry for him. He was falling apart right before my eyes. He started shaking his head uncontrollably again. Falling to his knees, he cradled the gun in his hand and looked up towards the sky.

Maybe he was praying and asking God to forgive him for what he had done to such a beautiful woman. I scooted to the edge of the couch and glanced down the hallway. I could see my bedroom door from where I was sitting on the couch and just as I stood to make a break for it, a single gunshot rang through my apartment. My eyes almost fell out of my head because my heart ceased beating momentarily as I took in what had just happened before I, too, fell to my knees and started to scream... and scream... and scream...

CHAPTER 25

"I am reporting live from Courtyard Manor where an attempted murder suicide has taken place. Witnesses say twenty three year old Naomi Duncan returned from work this afternoon where a gunman was waiting in her apartment. She was held hostage before the gunman turned the gun on himself. Naomi was not harmed. The gunman's name has not yet been released to the public. More news on this case will be reported as it becomes available. This is Haley O'Reilly reporting live..."

Cop cars and ambulances flooded my complex and yellow tape blocked off my apartment and three other condos to protect outsiders from the crime scene. As I sat in the back of the ambulance with a brown blanket wrapped around my shoulders, I was still shaking at the memory of Amos' suicide. Blood and brain fragments had stuck to my clothing making me sick to my stomach and I fought the urge to vomit. Although I wasn't hurt, the paramedics wanted to check me out to make sure I was okay. They refused to release me until a family member came to get me because I was in shock and traumatized by what I had just witnessed.

I closed my eyes as the scene replayed over and over again in my head. It was all I could see and I couldn't stop crying. When the back door to the ambulance opened and I saw Shauna and my father, I knew I was safe. I started sobbing loudly as Shauna jumped in and wrapped her arms around me.

"It's okay Naomi," she said rubbing my back. I could tell by her voice that she, too, was in tears. Knowing I was in danger was scary, but I wasn't sure if they realized how close to death I had been.

"Naomi, my baby girl," Daddy said coming over to me and kissing me on the forehead more times than I could count.

"I'm so so happy you're okay Naomi, you have no idea," Shauna said putting her hand on her chest.

"I'm happy to be alive. I thought I was going to die."

"Shauna called your boss and let her know what happened. She said take all the time you need. I'm going to go get you some clothes and you're going to come to my house and let Daddy take care of you. I'm not taking no for an answer," he said.

Daddy kissed my forehead again and I felt like I was 5 years old. The nightmare was over. Joe was dead and Daddy was there to scare away the boogeyman. The only thing I was worried about was Kamden and how I was going to explain how his uncle ended up dead in my apartment.

Daddy and Shauna sat in the ambulance with me while the police got ready to take Amos' body out of my apartment. Daddy was starting to get impatient so he went to talk to the cops to see how long it would be before he could get inside my apartment to get some of my belongings.

Shauna was rubbing my head softly in an attempt to relax me when the ambulance doors opened again. I was expecting to see my father climb back in, but it was Kamden and Big Momma staring inside. I was nervous because I didn't know what they thought was going on or how to even begin to explain it.

"I'm gonna go find out what's going on with Daddy," Shauna said kissing me on the forehead and climbing out of the ambulance to make room for Kamden. He climbed in and approached me, looking me up and down to make sure I didn't have any injuries. Hesitantly, he grabbed my hand and sat down next to me.

"How you feelin'?" He asked with a small smile.

"I'm alright, still a little shaken up."

Kamden nodded his head. I was trying to look in his eyes and figure out what he was thinking, but I wasn't getting anything.

"Ummm… I'm trying to figure out what to say because I'm shocked and confused about everything MiMi. I am."

I nodded my head because I could empathize with him. Losing two people who were like his parents so close together was already hard without adding in the fact his Uncle had committed suicide at my apartment.

"I'll tell you everything Kamden. I should've told you

from the beginning."

This time Kamden shook his head.

"You don't have to tell me anything MiMi, Big Momma already explained everything to me."

My mouth dropped open in shock.

"She told you…everything? All of it?"

"Yeah, everything. I know how my Uncle came on to you at his house and you turned him down. Big Momma thinks it was my Aunt Ginger's death that triggered something inside of him and he just got obsessed with you."

Speechless, I looked over at Big Momma who just nodded and winked at me as she clutched her brown purse.

"Yeah," I said nodding my head. "I should have told you, you were just going through so much and I didn't wanna stress you out."

"I understand, you don't have to apologize baby. It was nothing you did wrong. I'm the one that's sorry. You only met Uncle Amos because of me. I just had no idea all of this would happen-"

"It's okay Kamden, I don't blame you. We don't have to talk about it, I don't really want to anyway."

"Yeah Kamden, don't overwhelm her with all that right now. It has to be unpleasant for her."

Kamden kissed my hand without saying another word about it.

Shauna and my father came back to the ambulance to let me know they were going to go in to get my stuff as soon as they carried the body out. I nodded my head and squeezed Kamden's hand.

"Daddy, this is my boyfriend Kamden," I said softly. Kamden smiled and squeezed my hand back and I knew he was happy. He climbed out the truck so he could shake his hand.

"It's nice to meet you sir," he said respectfully. My father gave him a once over and a brief smile.

"Nice to meet you too, son. I heard a lot about you."

I didn't know what my father meant by that comment, so I just let it go. Kamden introduced my father to Big Momma and he shook her hand and gave her a bright smile, opposite of the one he had just given my boyfriend.

"Kamden, help an old woman in this truck. Why don't you go with her father and sister get her belongings, I'll sit with MiMi."

Kamden did as he was told and closed the ambulance doors.

"I got your letter a couple days ago," she said in a whisper as she shook her head. "I always knew that Amos was no damn good."

"You're not mad at me?"

"Mad at you for what? Because my daughter is dead? Why would I be mad at you when you didn't kill her? You had no way of knowing that Joe character was Ginger's husband."

"But he said he did it for me. I knew he was married when I started sleeping with him."

"*Survival.* Did you hear anything I said on Christmas? If I really believed for one second you told Amos to kill my daughter, I would've ran straight to the police station and told everything I thought I knew. You're not that type of person. My father used to always tell me I had a gift. I could tell spot on if a person had a good heart or not, and I could tell the second you walked in my kitchen your heart was loving and pure. That's why I like you. Only a good woman with a sincere heart can have a man jumping through loopholes like you have my grandson doing. *You* did not kill Ginger, so I don't want to hear another word about it. As far as anybody knows Amos got obsessed with you after the death of his wife. I burned that letter you sent me, and I'm taking that secret with me to the grave."

"You're never going to tell anyone Amos killed Ginger?'"

She hesitated for a minute before she answered that question.

"I thought about it, but what good would it do?" Big Momma asked rhetorically, shrugging her shoulders. "Ginger is not going to come back and that's really all I want. I don't want my daughter to be remembered for the way she died… I want her to be remembered for the way she lived."

Hearing Big Momma say that had me wondering what people would remember about me when I was dead and gone. I didn't want it to be for the way I used men to feel good about myself or what purse I was carrying. I wanted to be remembered for the heart Big Momma said I had…loving and pure… all of the things I had never taken the time to portray because of the hurt I'd always felt people put on me, starting with my Momma leaving us.

After all the things I'd done and the way I had devalued myself I didn't know why I was getting another chance, but I was grateful for it. Maybe this was confirmation that Kamden and I were meant to be together. There had been so many things that should have torn us apart, yet we were still together and more in love than ever. I couldn't think of anybody else in the world I wanted to be with. Although Kamden had cheated and hurt me, doing it back to him didn't make things any better for me in the end. If I felt so hurt and betrayed I should've left and since I'd made the choice to stay I had to let the past be the past. Yes, he had cheated on me... but at the end of the day I was cheating on him too and what goes around always comes right back around.

I wouldn't just walk away from this incident ignorant though, I had learned my lesson about using people and lying to those I loved. It would only leave everybody hurt, confused, in danger... even dead.

CHAPTER 26

"I'm glad you had a chance to stop by," Kapri said handing me a glass of wine. "You know I'm still worried about you."

"I know. It's been so hectic getting the things out of my apartment and going to therapy."

"Yeah I understand. How have you been though? Since everything happened?"

"It's been hard, but I'm just taking it day by day. My family has been so supportive...and you. Almost overbearing."

"We're supposed to be. You were almost killed Naomi! I am so glad you were unharmed. I don't know what the hell I would do if something happened to you. You're my best friend, and you know I could never get another one because I don't trust females."

I laughed because she was telling the absolute truth.

"You don't have to worry, I'm not going anywhere for a long time."

"How long are you going to therapy?" Kapri asked getting some grapes out of her refrigerator and sitting back down across from me at her small, wooden dining room table.

"I don't know. I'll probably keep going, just not every week like I have been. At least once a month. You'd be surprised how much it helps to talk to someone who can help you sort your feelings out."

"Maybe I'll give it a try."

"What's going on with you and Brock? Are you still seeing him?" I asked taking a hefty sip of wine.

Kapri tried not to, but she couldn't help the huge smile that had spread across her face.

"Yes, we are still together and it's actually getting serious, that's another reason I wanted you to come over today."

She took a pause, looking at me like she had taken the last cookie from the cookie jar.

"I'm pregnant," she announced.

"WHAT? Oh my gosh, are you serious?" I asked in total disbelief. I had not seen this one coming.

"Yes girl. I know I still can't believe it."

"That's why you haven't poured yourself a glass of wine and you're sitting in here nibbling on that fruit."

"And after over ten years of friendship you didn't even notice. I'm disappointed in you."

We both laughed.

"Well how do you feel, are you excited? What did Brock say? Have you told your parents?"

"One question at a time Naomi," she said laughing. "I am... still shocked but I'm actually happy. Brock was ecstatic which shocked the hell outta me. And my parents are already talking about getting a passport like they're really just about to be taking my baby out of the country."

"How far along are you?"

"Only about six weeks, so I have a long way to go... and you know you're godmommy."

"I better be! And I better be maid of honor at you and Brock's wedding."

"Hold your horses now, nobody said anything about marriage, let's take it one major life event at a time."

Kapri and I talked about her future plans for the baby, names and my plans to finish school and get my degree in law. After all the negative, there was so much positive stuff going on in everybody's life. I was so happy to be alive to witness it.

Pulling into Kamden's driveway I turned my car off and grabbed my purse and the deep dish pizza I'd picked up on the way. Using my key, I walked into the house where he was sitting on the couch watching Game of Thrones. I kicked off my shoes and grabbed the pizza box before cuddling up next to him and grabbing a slice.

I'd spent some time at my Daddy's house after everything happened, but I already knew I never wanted to go back to that apartment. Not only was it where Joe had ended his life, it held too many memories of him and my past. Kamden suggested I stay with him until I found a place, but once I moved in, I never started looking and the fact that I woke up one morning with a key to his house on the nightstand next to my purse showed me he was fine with that.

"Guess who's pregnant?"

"You?" he asked and I couldn't tell if his voice was scared or hopeful.

"No, Kapri. She's six weeks."

"That's cool. She excited about that?"

"Yeah she is. And of course I'm the Godmommy so that makes you Goddaddy."

Kamden laughed.

"Did you tell Kapri? I know she aint feeling that."

"She's warming up to you."

I ate more pizza and watched TV with Kamden for a couple hours before we went to bed. I laid on top of him and he wrapped his arms around me.

"Don't be surprised if I wake you up in the middle of the night to get some," he whispered in my ear.

"Don't be surprised if I'm up waiting."

I awoke the next morning to someone banging on the door. I swear the house was shaking and I jumped up immediately, shaking Kamden out of his sleep.

"Kamden, what's that? Who is at the door?"

He jumped up, threw on some sweats and retrieved his gun from underneath the mattress.

"Stay right here."

He left the room quickly and I sat in the bed for only a minute before I too got up, put on my robe and left to see what the hell was going on. My Daddy always did tell me I never followed directions.

When I walked into the living room I could hear Kamden talking to someone, although I couldn't see who it was. I couldn't make out what they were saying, so I crept closer to the door so I could hear what was going on.

"Where is she? I know she's in there," a woman said.

"Look, you need to tell me what the hell is going on or get off my doorstep-"

"Go get her! I just wanna talk to her for a second."

"Who are you talking about?"

"MiMi! Go get her, I know she's in there."

Hearing enough, I hurried to the door to see which one of Kamden's bitches had shown up at his door trying to check me. As soon as I made it to the door though my mouth completely went dry and I didn't know what to say or do. Really, I needed to pinch myself to make sure I wasn't still asleep because I could not be looking at the person that was standing in front of me. Clearing my throat and swallowing, I opened my mouth to say her name because that was the only way I would believe it was real.

"Momma?" I asked, and I sounded exactly like the little girl I'd been the last time I saw her.

"MiMi," she said like she used to when I was little, her eyes filled with tears. My Daddy used to tell me the only reason she'd named me Naomi was so she could nickname me MiMi.

We both just stood there staring at each other in disbelief. She had aged since I'd last seen her, but not too much. Her hair was still brown, although most of the strands in the front had been replaced by gray ones. She was dressed in black slacks and a red and black sweater and thigh high boots. She didn't look rich, but I could certainly tell she wasn't hurting for money which raised my suspicions through the roof.

"I saw you on the news, I'm so glad you're okay," she said.

"Where the fuck have you been all these years?" I asked stepping in front of Kamden and ignoring her comment. My emotions were all over the place, but seeing her standing before me completely healthy was infuriating me.

"Baby, I know you have questions and I wanna answer all of them. There is so much you don't know."

"No, I know that you left me and Shauna. You acted like you were going to the store one morning and you never came back."

"I would've never left you and your sister, it's not like that. I went to the store that day and got the milk. I didn't come back because your father tried to kill me."

I glanced at Kamden and then back to the woman who birthed me, was this all some sort of prank? Was my life built on a foundation of distrust?

ABOUT THE AUTHOR

DeQuindra Renea is a 26 year old Flint Michigan native. She attends school full time at the University of Michigan-Flint and works as a middle and high school substitute teacher. She has been writing since the sixth grade. In her free time DeQuindra likes to play with her daughter, spend time with family and friends, cook, and sing karoke. Blazing Deception is her first novel.